A
COMMUNITY
OF
WRITERS

A Collection of Short Stories

EDITED BY
ANN ELIA STEWART

A COMMUNITY OF WRITERS

For information about special discounts for bulk purchases, please contact Sunbury Press, Inc. Wholesale Dept. at (717) 254-7274 or orders@sunburypress.com.

To request one of our authors for speaking engagements or book signings, please contact Sunbury Press, Inc. Publicity Dept. at publicity@sunburypress.com.

FIRST SUNBURY PRESS EDITION
Printed in the United States of America
April 2012

Trade Paperback ISBN: 978-1-620060-49-0
Mobipocket format (Kindle) ISBN: 978-1-620060-50-6
ePub format (Nook) ISBN: 978-1-620060-51-3

Published by:
Sunbury Press
Camp Hill, PA
www.sunburypress.com

Camp Hill, Pennsylvania   USA

"Everybody's life is full of stories. . .what is interesting is the way everyone tells their stories."
Gertrude Stein

INTRODUCTION

For ten years I have had the pleasure of facilitating a creative writing workshop at the Fredricksen Library in Camp Hill, Pennsylvania. It began as a complement to a literary magazine I had been publishing at the time, *PHASE,* which at the end of its run, had published fifty central Pennsylvania authors (selected over time from five hundred submitted manuscripts). I was searching for new voices, interesting stories for the magazine, and I had been noticing writers making some of the same mistakes in those five hundred manuscripts that most first-time authors make when they put pen to paper (or fingers to keyboard).

The repetition of mistakes led me to create a writing workshop that addressed them, but also allowed for creative discussion and expression. The goal I set for each class was to try to polish a story to the point of confidence: continue to work on the story outside of the workshop, form writing and critique groups, pick up a book or two from the recommended reading list distributed at every workshop, and work at the craft.

Only then can a writer begin to send his or her babies out into the world to the myriad literary magazines, many of them now on-line, or develop a short story into a novella or novel.

In 2003, word of the workshop had reached Robert Craumer, a Camp Hill resident who was seeking a way to memorialize his beloved wife, Natalie, who had succumbed to cancer. Natalie had been a voracious reader, having read her way through four libraries, and having penned a few articles and short stories herself. Mr. Craumer set his sight on his hometown library and learned more about the writing workshop. He had decided that not only was this a perfect way to honor his wife, but it would further her love of stories by giving education and opportunity to other aspiring central Pennsylvania writers.

The Natalie D. Craumer Writer's Workshop at the Fredricksen Library in Camp Hill was born. Offered free to the community, it is a workshop comprised of a maximum of fifteen participants, some of whom have become familiar faces over the years. The workshop, offered in the fall and the spring, always fills quickly. And whether it is because of the camaraderie that is encouraged in each session, the wealth of information and discussion, and the participants' willingness to complete assignments — or all three — the stories that emerge always overwhelm me in their breadth of creativity, voice and structure.

Here are twenty-five stories, written by workshop participants from nearly every year, many of whom have gone on to win competitions, publish their stories in literary journals, and even write and publish novels. The stories were either developed, or grew from seeds planted during the workshop. The writing levels represent intermediate to advanced, and each story is vibrant and engaging without the distractions of heavy-handed philosophy and stylistic tricks. The stories pull you in, and in some cases, teach you something about life. They also range from mainstream to literary fiction to fantasy, science fiction and satire.

To say that I am proud of each of "my" writers is an understatement. Their passion for story led them to the workshop, but their dedication to work at their craft landed them within the pages of this anthology as well as other publications.

A huge thank you to Lawrence Knorr, publisher, Sunbury Press, Camp Hill, Pennsylvania, who recognized the little gem that is the Natalie D.

Craumer Writer's Workshop at the Fredricksen Library. All profits from the sale of this book will be donated to the library so that the written word can continue to be enjoyed by all who walk through its doors.

Thank you, Mr. Craumer, for your belief in and support of creative writing. Thank you, Fredricksen Library, for offering the workshop twice a year and giving us a home. Thank you, Lee Johnson, for suggesting the workshop in the first place! Thank you, Jessica Nupponen, the library's community events director, for your excellent support in all things administrative: registration, scheduling, materials and the endless handout copies of which I never seem to run out. You have been my right arm. And thank you, writers, for hanging in there, exercising your minds, and crafting these excellent short stories.

Enjoy!
Ann Elia Stewart
Workshop facilitator

Hunting Season

By
Rayne Ayers Debski

It's almost midnight when Andrew maneuvers our car up the serpentine road to the Sanctuary. Without street lights to illuminate the curves, the abrupt shifts are unexpected. My back stiffens in preparation for the next one. Andrew swings the car hard enough for my shoulder to knock against the door. I'm too tired to complain; he's too intent on getting to our destination to notice. We were supposed to be there five hours ago. Andrew had to work late.

Sanctuary is a misnomer. Our vacation home in the Blue Ridge sits on a half acre of trees, among dozens like it. We selected the name because that's what we wanted: Andrew, a getaway from his accounting firm, and me, a place to bring environmental magazines and Terra chips. We haven't been here since the summer when the forest hid everything. Now, in October, leaves pile along the road.

"Did you tell Jake to turn on the heat?"

I shake my head. "I thought we'd build a fire." I imagined we would sit in front of the fireplace, watch logs spit out insects, and plan what to do during a long weekend together. It seemed more exciting than calling the caretaker to start the furnace.

"We'll be getting into a cold bed."

"I thought we'd dance naked in front of the fire."

"We've never done that."

"I never ate mussels until I met you." This is a game we play, a reminder of "firsts" we've shared during our nine years together, a game of truth and lies. Usually, my husband responds with something like "I never farted in silk boxers before I met you." Tonight he stares at the road ahead.

"Did you remember to buy fruit?" He turns the car into our driveway. "I didn't put it on the shopping list."

1

"Blueberries," I say. "And bananas."

He reaches for my hand and squeezes it. This affectionate gesture belies the distance that has grown between us.

"Are you okay?" He still holds my damp hand.

"Fine." I remove myself from his grasp and gather my things. In the last year we've gone to cooking classes, cleaned out the basement, taken up digital photography. We joke. We share stories with friends. We rarely look each other in the eye. "You?"

"Yes," he says.

We are here in the mountains with its bracing air and snakes in the laundry room to have three days without anyone else.

He locks the car. "I'm fine."

By dawn, barn swallows are singing. Sleep is impossible. With a blanket around my shoulders, I walk through the kitchen onto the mildewed wooden deck.

I scan the tops of the yellow hickories for the Orionids. Last year we stayed awake all night to see the meteor showers. The luminous streaks we'd read about—meteors every five minutes!—never appeared. Instead of going to bed, Andrew insisted we return to Richmond so he could ride with his bicycle club. We drove home in silence. This morning I watch a single meteor streak across the sky. From its position, I know it's not part of the Orionids. Maybe I'll tell Andrew it was. Slowly, the sky lightens.

Dressed for his daily run in new shorts and an old sweat shirt, Andrew slides open the door to the deck. "Do you want hot water for tea?" Without waiting for an answer, he fills the kettle. His six-foot muscular presence shrinks the space in the kitchen. The blender pulverizes bananas, orange juice, and yogurt. Jays bicker in the trees. I must remember to buy birdseed. A piece of blue cloth I shoved into the screen the last time we were here has turned dark green.

He pours his smoothie into a glass and gulps it down. Although he has recently turned forty, there's no gray in his thick, dark hair. The creases in his forehead are recent,

2

etched from worries about his firm's survivability. He pokes his head out the door. "Water's ready."

"When will you be back?"

"You can come with me if you want."

"I don't feel like running."

"Too wet out?"

"I feel like I'll use up too much of myself. I've been feeling that way. Used. Used up."

"Maybe you need new running shoes."

"New running shoes?"

"You can tell your friends 'I sprinted past my husband in my new Nikes.'"

"I'd never sprint past you. I can't even keep up with you."

He squints at the glass wind chime, his anniversary gift to me, its strands twisted into silence. "You should have brought that inside."

"Sometimes things get away from me." One of the bickering jays swoops toward the deck, then returns to its mate. "What do you want me to do?"

"I'm not asking you to do anything." He unhooks the wind chime and hands it to me. The glass is cold and slippery. "Just wish you'd take better care of things."

I place the chimes on the picnic table and unravel the strings. I'm not a careless person. I may overlook the expiration date on a milk carton or mail a payment the day it's due. But at the Piedmont Historical Society, where I'm the Executive Director, every object is correctly identified. Our home in Richmond is not a showplace, but the gardens are weeded. And here in the mountains, I sweep away spider webs and keep the wine rack filled. If something is amiss, it isn't, as Andrew insists, because of negligence. After all these years, he still doesn't understand there are things I do because of carelessness, but others I do for spite.

My bare feet are turning blue. Andrew is at least a mile into his run. The jays have quieted. I re-hang the wind chime but go inside before it begins to sing.

There is laughter from the neighbor's yard, my husband's loud and nasal, and Kit Barton's, low and throaty. From the kitchen window I can almost see the house next door. The Bartons moved here last spring. Unlike us, they live on the mountain year round. Kit Barton is an expert bow hunter, and Mark Barton is the owner of a private fishing club. He's a potential client of Andrew's firm. If they're outside when Andrew finishes his run, he talks with them. His chattiness with strangers irritates me—I hate feeling excluded. I run upstairs to his study for binoculars, as if they'll help me hear what he's saying to Kit.

After rummaging through his closet, knocking over the twelve-gauge shotgun and spilling a box of ammunition, I find the binoculars. By the time I place them around my neck, Andrew is in the doorway.

"The Bartons invited us for dinner tonight." He picks at his fingernail. "I said we'd be there."

Moments like this lead me to believe our marriage has become a game of Blind Man's Bluff. If I remind him this is our weekend to be alone together, he'll look baffled. I hold up the binoculars. "Bird watching. I thought we could look for eagles."

He shakes his head. "Five o'clock. Don't be late."

Come early for drinks, the Bartons told Andrew, so we can get to know Susan.

"If they don't like me, will they send us on our way without dinner?"

Andrew roots around the wine rack. Although I can't see his face, I know he's wincing. He has never enjoyed what he calls my overactive imagination. "Better fill up on hors d'oeuvres just in case."

"Maybe they'll drug us. Use us as decoys to lure wild animals." The inanity of my words shields my nervousness about hanging with people who will judge Andrew by his wife. I hadn't thought to bring anything dressier than jeans and a sweater. I try to dislodge a tiny piece of dried steak from the sweater with my fingernail.

"Bison burgers," he says getting into the spirit. "That's what they'll serve. Fresh from the hunt." He sets out a zinfandel and a cabernet, sizing up which would be the correct choice.

"Five o'clock is early for dinner."

"Kit wants us to see the sunset."

"Something different from what we see here?"

He holds each bottle to the light and examines its color. "Pretend you're Eve, seeing a sunset for the first time."

"I bet Eve didn't eat buffalo. Or deer." I scrape harder. "Or ostrich." The meat disappears from my sweater, but a small star of balsamic glaze remains. I rearrange my scarf to cover it.

"You don't know that." He places the wine in a tote and hands it to me. "But I'm with you on the ostrich." I grab some nuts to chew while we walk next door. Maybe tonight won't be so bad. We'll listen to their stories and joke about them afterward. I turn to offer some nuts to Andrew, but he's out the door. I rinse my hands and leave the wine on the counter.

It takes a few seconds to catch up to him. "Let's not ruin this weekend," I say.

He slows his pace. "This weekend?" His face is drawn. "Is that all you're worried about?"

Heads of glassy-eyed animals cover the walls of the Barton's living room. A deer with a rack large enough to decorate at Christmas stares disapprovingly at my sweater. I tug at my scarf. Next to him is an antelope, his tilted head exuding disdain. Three elk eye the room as if looking for an escape route. Above them float a tarpon and four bass. I try to avoid their gazes and smell what's for dinner; the burning wood in the fireplace displaces all other scents.

"The animals are Kit's," Mark says. "The fish are mine. Caught the tarpon off Key Largo." His voice is quiet, as if he doesn't want to rile the animals. I press my lips together and pretend to be interested.

From a group of pictures on the sideboard, he selects one and hands it to me. "She spent seven hours lying in the mud to get the elk," he says proudly. I hold the photo like a piece of smelly underwear and glance at the picture of Kit in dirt covered camouflage, her bow in one hand, her foot atop the carcass, a patch of rust stained grass in the foreground. I hope dinner isn't the remains of this animal.

"Seven hours." I fight the urge to toss the picture into the fire. "I couldn't lay that long in a spa." Andrew shoots me a warning look.

Kit continues the tour. Next to the stone fireplace, a five foot bear skin is spread across the wall. "She was six years old," Kit says nodding at the bear as if eulogizing it. "I shot her in Canada." Her diamond earrings sparkle. I turn to Andrew hoping he's as uncomfortable as I am and willing to leave.

"Did you have a sidearm with you?" my husband asks.

Kit's chestnut hair swings across her shoulders. "They're not permitted in Canada when you're bow hunting."

"What if you missed and the bear charged?"

She shrugs. "That's the chance you take." Her white silk shirt ripples. "Do you hunt?"

"We shoot skeet," I say. Andrew looks as if one of the trophies has joined the conversation.

He turns to Kit. "I used to bow hunt. Mostly deer."

"You should come with us," she says. "Bow season starts next week. We're driving up to the game lands."

"We're only here for a couple of days," I say.

"I'd like to try my hand at bow hunting again." Andrew smiles at Kit and me, his head bobbling back and forth. "Susan keeps trying to get me up here more." The bobbling has changed to a definite nod. "Yes. Next weekend."

Before I can protest, Mark presses a glass into my hand. I rarely drink more than a glass of wine on an empty stomach. I swallow three cosmos in succession before Mark ushers us into the dining room. He's saying something about their last fishing trip, "...and guess how many bass I caught that afternoon. Guess."

I shake my head. "I have no idea."

"Andrew, what do you think? How many?"

Andrew's eyes search the table. "The wine," he says. "What did you do with the wine?"

I raise my fingers to my lips and try to look contrite. "I never left a bottle of wine at home until I met you."

Andrew hisses into my ear. "You're drunk." I busy myself with my napkin so no one will see the flush spreading across my face.

"Would you believe a dozen?" Mark says.

Kit sets a plate in front of each of us. The last thing I remember is the empty eyes of trout staring up at me.

In the morning Andrew and I occupy the kitchen and avoid eye contact. He starts the water for my tea, opens the refrigerator and sniffs the cold, fusty air escaping into the room. I stare at a croissant deciding if it's worth the effort to eat it. A brown paper bag sits on the counter, its smell revealing the contents of leftover trout from last night's dinner. Andrew shoves the bag into the trash and carries it to the porch.

"Do you want to go for a hike later?" He thrusts a box of herbal teabags on the table.

"Aren't you hunting with your friends?" I jab strawberry preserves into the croissant. When I take a bite, crushed red fruit oozes down the side of my mouth. I grab a napkin, hoping he hasn't noticed what a mess I'm making.

A cloud of steam rises from the water he pours into my teacup. "Sun's out. It's not cold." He drinks his smoothie straight from the blender carafe. "Do you want to hike or not?"

I shake my head. A slice of sunlight cuts the kitchen in two. On one side I sit hunched in my chair, wool sweater buttoned to my throat, bare feet pressed against the floor. He could walk across the kitchen, touch my hair, and the day would be different. He remains at the counter, a hulking presence stuffing granola bars into his running shorts.

"Maybe I'll shoot skeet." I try to chuckle so he'll know I'm joking, but it comes out like a gurgle. He's too busy filling his water bottle to notice.

"Suit yourself." The thick hair on his arms bristles when he opens the door. "Make sure you put the trash in the shed."

My head aches from last night's alcohol. I open the door to the deck to let air into the room. Too fatigued to read the morning paper, I make a pillow with my arms on the table and rest my head. Almost asleep, I imagine hiking to the mountaintop and sitting there, waiting for Andrew to find me. It's the kind of thing he used to do—guide our canoe

7

through white water, talk me down steep ski slopes. That was when he wasn't so distant, before he started going on camping trips without me, before he started locking the glove box of his car, before he started making excuses for not calling when he worked late.

A breeze blows against the wind chimes. I'm unsure how much time has passed. The tea is cold; I make a fresh cup. Outside, the bushes rustle. Something strikes the side of the house, a branch, perhaps. It's not unusual for birds to fly into open windows or raccoons to saunter onto the deck for a handout.

Gripping the cup with both hands, I sip my tea. Although the erratic thumping continues, I refuse to let my "overactive imagination" take hold. It's probably a deer. I peruse the newspaper headlines.

A musty odor blows into the house. Remembering the discarded trout, I stiffen. The trash can crashes against the door. I swing around.

The shadow of a six-foot bear crosses the deck. I fling the mug toward him and half run, half stumble up the narrow circular staircase to Andrew's study. I try to still my hands long enough to lock the door.

I scrunch down on the floor, my head pounding. Shit. Why didn't I grab the cell phone?

Below me, glass shatters. I close my eyes and cling to the side of the cold leather sofa. In his search for food, the bear is having his way with my kitchen, riffling cabinets and tossing plates. I have to get to the shotgun in the closet. I crawl across the carpet.

A chair scrapes the tile floor. I envision the bear sitting at the pine table waiting for me to feed him. I glance at the clock. Andrew should have returned by now. I think of the bear tramping through the woods. Would Andrew have seen him? What if the bear found him first? I imagine my husband running on the trail, the sun casting a golden glow around his head. Even the thick hair on his arms seems luminous. His quadriceps throb, the muscles hardening and thickening. The bear lunges for him, crushes Andrew's heaving torso between his paws, and tears at his clothes. He rips the granola bar from Andrew and tosses his damaged body to the ground like an empty soda bottle. What if Andrew is bleeding in the woods awaiting help? No. He's probably at the Barton's discussing their hunting plans for next weekend.

A rumbling belch echoes through the house. My mouth is dry; sweat pours down my sides. The bear will sniff my fear. He'll rip my heart out.

I pull the shotgun from the closet and pray my shaking will stop so I can load it and aim straight.

I creep to the landing and huddle behind the stair rail. The sun is so intense now it distorts my vision. My head throbs. The hulking figure is silhouetted against the windows overlooking the forest. He moves closer. Our eyes meet.

In that moment we recognize something familiar in each other. He gives a guilty shrug, and for a fierce instant I want to bury myself in him, forgive him for everything he has done. We stare at each other. I inhale, raise the gun, and take aim. The pounding in my head blurs my vision. He shakes his head.

I lower the weapon and close my eyes, knowing he will do with me what he wants. Outside, trees rustle and wind chimes sing softly in the breeze.

Rayne Debski's short stories have appeared in literary journals, anthologies, and e-zines, and have been selected for readings by professional theatre groups in New York and Philadelphia. She can occasionally be found on the Six Sentences blog. She wishes her muse would visit more frequently.

TAKE CARE

BY
MARGARET DEANGELIS

Susan had the idea when she got a letter from Greg Campbell and a boy she knew in high school on the same day a month before school started. She wasn't surprised to hear from Greg. He told her he was joining the army and he told her he'd write. The letter from Robert, the boy from high school, was a surprise, and if he hadn't mentioned POD class she might not have been able to place him. He was the boy who sat in front of her and had a stammer that got worse when he had to give an answer. Mostly she remembered how patient their teacher was, and how she wanted to be like that when she was a teacher.

She got some names from her pastor and from the campus chaplain, and the other girls in her prayer group got some too. Since they got back to campus in September they have been meeting each week to pray for all the boys over there. On their own they pray for one or two boys specifically and write them letters. Susan prays for Greg and for Robert Hughes, the boy she knew in high school. She writes to Greg twice a week, but to Robert only once a month or so. The letters to him are shorter and less personal than the ones she writes to Greg because she doesn't remember him very well.

The chaplain calls what Susan and the girls are doing a ministry, and that made it sound so important that she bought special papers just for this. The kind she uses for the letters to Greg comes in a box of twenty-five decorated sheets, five plain sheets, and twenty-five envelopes. The paper is thin and crinkly and printed with rosebuds. It has a fragrance card wrapped in cellophane that you are supposed to open and slip between the sheets, but she hasn't done that. The paper is too thin to use both sides, so she has learned to write small so that she can say a lot.

She is half way through the second box and has three undecorated sheets from the first box left.

The paper she uses for Robert's letters is plain, not as thin as the Greg paper and with a slightly slubbed texture. It comes in gummed pads. The envelopes are packaged separately and she doesn't have to be so careful to match the number of sheets to the number of envelopes. Because she has less to say to Robert she makes her handwriting slightly larger, so that she can often use two sheets and the letters look like more than what they are.

The letters follow a pattern. She begins with where she is while she is writing. ("I'm at the front desk of the dorm on phone duty tonight." "I'm upstairs at the Rat before I go to European Novels of the 20th Century.") She talks about the weather, about the authors she's reading and the papers she has to write. She gives Greg news about people he knows on campus but she doesn't tell Robert those things because it wouldn't mean anything to him. Sometimes she reports that she's gone to a movie ("They showed *The Birds* again on Saturday night." "We went downtown to see *The Graduate*. I bought the album.") but she doesn't say that she's gone with a boy from her creative writing class or her friend's older brother. Sometimes she comments on things Greg or Robert have written to her. ("Sounds like you guys did your best to have a Merry Christmas." "I like the names for your scout dogs. We had a Blackie when I was little.")

She mentions the war only obliquely when she ends each letter, "Greg (or Robert), you take care." On Robert's she puts just her name, but Greg's she signs, "Love, Susan." She's not sure what she means by that. She likes Greg a lot and she cares for him in a way that is more meaningful than the way she cares for Robert, of whom she has only hazy memories of his round face and his stammer. If he had not written to her she probably would never have thought of him unless he came to their class reunion, still two years away. She would have thought of Greg even if she hadn't heard from him, of the way he touched her knee during the gunfire at the end of *Bonnie and Clyde*, the way he kissed her on the cheek at the door of her dorm.

She has not written to either boy since before spring vacation. She is on phone duty again tonight. The phone isn't ringing much but it is too noisy in the lobby of the dorm for her to concentrate on Sartre's *Nausea*, whose main character she finds boring and whiny. She wonders if his self-absorption might sound better in French and regrets, albeit briefly, that she took German so she could be in the same class with a tall, handsome aspiring journalist named Dan who transferred to another school after one semester, before she had a chance to get to know him.

She takes out two undecorated sheets of what she thinks of as the Greg paper.

"April 17, 1968, Dear Greg," she begins.

"Sorry I haven't written for almost three weeks. Over Easter break I went with Tracy (the girl I told you about that I did the diagramming of "The Silken Tent" with for Dr. Price) to her family's house on Long Beach Island. It was too cold to go in the water, of course, but walking along the beach was nice when it wasn't windy. I'm sending you a stone I picked up on one of my walks. Archibald MacLeish says that what you see when you hold a stone in your hand is what has fallen out of the water. The water and the stone come together and separate, come together and separate. The little white patch in the crease of the stone caught my eye. While I was walking I was saying the names of all you boys over there that I pray for and I had just said your name when I saw the sun catch the white patch as the tide went out. It reminded me of the white patch of hair behind your right ear, the patch I saw every day when you sat in front of me in Ed Psych. You turned around one day to ask me if I knew Dr. Huzzard's office hours and I said, 'Do you know you have a little patch of white hair behind your right ear?' That was the first thing I ever said to you. I remembered that when I saw the stone. I picked it up and carried it in my shirt pocket for the rest of the time I was there. I thought you might like to have it, to think of me when you touch it, and remember that I'm praying for you.

"I think Tracy and I are going to live at the beach house this summer and work at Playland. Her brother is graduating and in the fall he'll be teaching at Long Beach

High, like he always wanted, and we're going to fix the house up so he can live there all year.

"That's all for tonight. I have to work on a paper about Hebrew mysticism for Dr. Spotts's class. It's really interesting stuff.

"Greg, you take care.

"Love, Susan"

She slips the stone and the letter, which she has written on two of the undecorated sheets of the Greg paper, into a padded envelope. The glue has a sour taste, and when she presses the flap down hard to seal it, she can feel some of the bubbles in the padding pop, as they did when she wrote the address on the front. She will have to take this to the mail room tomorrow to have it weighed for the proper postage.

She sets the envelope aside and draws out the last undecorated sheet from the first box of Greg paper. She chooses another stone from the bag she has brought back from the beach. This one is round with some orange streaks. She turns it over several times. Then she picks up her pen again.

"April 17, 1968. Dear Robert," she begins.

Margaret DeAngelis is a lifelong resident of central Pennsylvania. After a long teaching career, she left the classroom to devote herself to developing as a fiction writer. She has attended the Bread Loaf Writers' Conference, the Sewanee Writers' Conference, and has received fellowships from the Jentel Artist Residency, the Vermont Studio Center, and the Hambidge Center.

ANGEL IN THE MIST

BY
LAURIE J. EDWARDS

Annie O'Brien hurried along the gangplank, hunger and fear clawing at her belly. A solid wall of wood towered before her, gleaming in the sunlight. How could such a huge steamer stay afloat, especially once the crowd, shuffling along behind her, boarded?

Yesterday this long-awaited trip to America had seemed an exciting dream. Had she, of all her siblings, been chosen to go? Annie had no need to pinch herself to be sure; her younger brother Seamus had administered a swift kick to her ankle, which still smarted. Now this morning's tiny ration of cornmeal mush curdled in her stomach, and thoughts of Seamus filled her with homesickness.

On deck the freshening breeze stung her cheeks and snapped the flags against the poles overhead, jingling iron rings on the ropes holding them aloft. The clanging metal reminded her of gaol gates slamming shut, caging her inside a prison. Drawing in a ragged breath, she struggled to still the quivering that shook her body as they steamed out to sea.

Suddenly, being a housemaid in America did not seem a wonderful future. Annie longed to lay her head on Mam's aproned lap, to feel the work-roughened hands stroking her hair. What if she never saw Mam or Da again? America was so far away. She tried to comfort herself that all the money she earned would buy food to keep her family alive. The shriveled, blackened potatoes could not. Baby Norah had died of hunger in Mam's arms. Old folks, like Gran, hands gnarled, bodies hunched, lay curled on pallets in low-roofed cottages awaiting death. And she, Annie, was to be their savior. She would work hard, send her pay back to feed first her family and later the village. Grandiose dreams, yes, but Annie had a mission. And succeed at it she would.

As the gulf grew between ship and land, the emerald grass of her beloved Ireland hazed into the distance in a blur of tears. Annie imprinted every detail of the coastline on her heart. She clutched the rail, straining to make out the sliver of shoreline on the horizon. When not a speck remained, she stumbled below deck to find her bunk.

Never had Annie glimpsed such a room. The ceiling rose higher than the thatched roof of her house, and beds were stacked one above the other. If Annie stood with arms outstretched, she could touch both sets of bunks.

The first few women to enter spoke only in whispers, and the silence hurt Annie's ears. The ship shuddering under her feet seemed a poor substitute for the laughing and squabbling of her brothers and sisters. Shortly, though, the room filled with mothers of squalling infants and whining toddlers, making Annie feel more at home. But that night, tucked under the coarse woolen blanket, Annie feared crashing to the floor as the ship dipped and rolled.

After breakfast Annie stood on deck, gazing back toward home. Then she strained forward to catch a glimpse of her future.

A shout startled her from her reveries. A red-faced girl holding a baby chased a runaway boy. The wiry, freckle-faced boy barreled into Annie, who caught him and twirled him around the way she did her younger brothers. He squealed and begged her to do it again.

"Thank you for catching him." The girl, not much older than Annie herself, puffed out a breath as she reached them. "I'm Frieda, the Luddingtons' nanny." The baby she balanced on her hip stared somberly from one to the other.

The boy muscled his way between them. "She's not our real nanny," he informed Annie. "Papa only hired her to take care of us 'til we get back to New York. Bridget couldn't come on this trip. She had to stay home on Long Island with Mama." With his hands clasped behind his back as if he were a connoisseur studying a painting, he examined Annie. "I'm Joseph Luddington the Third. Who are you?"

"Joseph," Frieda said sharply, "mind your manners."

Annie hid her smile at the young boy's aristocratic manner and made a mock curtsey. "Annie O'Brien, at your service."

"You have red curls like our Bridget," Joseph said. "Maybe Mama would hire you too."

Annie smiled. "I already have a job. The Duvalls paid my passage, so I must work for them." When Joseph's brows drew together, she added, "Perhaps later I could come to live with you."

Joseph studied her a moment longer. "Do you play marbles?"

"Sure, and don't I play with my brothers?" Not often. Chores usually took up most of the day, but she could shoot with the best of them.

Joseph took her hand and led her to a stateroom larger and more splendid than the chapel in her village. Two poodles raced toward them yipping. Joseph hugged each in turn. He dismissed Annie's exclamations with a wave of his hand. "My daddy's very 'portant. He went to England to 'stablish a new bank."

They sat crosslegged beside the marble sunburst on the foyer floor. Annie, who had only ever played with gray clay pellets, stared open-mouthed as Joseph poured a swirl of rainbow-colored glass from a leather pouch. But as she often did with her younger brothers, she let him beat her occasionally.

A splintering crash followed by a clanging bell startled Annie from sleep. Feet pounded up the stairs on the other side of the wall. Doors slammed. Screams and shouts echoed in the metal passageway. Clad only in her sleep shift and clutching her reticule, Annie struggled down from her upper berth as the ship floor lurched first one way, then the other. Hanging tightly to the handrail, she pulled herself up the stairs after the stampeding crowd.

A man seized Annie as she rushed onto the deck. He shoved her through the crowd. "Here's another young one."

Rough hands grabbed her and pushed her right arm into a boxy cork vest. Her reticule dropped to the deck when a man grabbed the other side of the life vest and thrust her left arm through the hole. Annie's stomach roiled, and she shivered in the wintery air.

She sucked in a breath so she wouldn't cry out as a deckhand held her over the side. Waves lapped against the hull, sending the lifeboat below bobbing. What if she missed and went plunging into the ocean?

A baby's cry startled her. Annie looked over her shoulder. The nanny, clutching baby Sarah to her chest, hustled Joseph along. "Please," she pleaded, "let us through."

"It's too late. This boat is full. One more person could sink it."

The nanny's voice shrilled in fear, "The next one then."

"That's the last one, miss," the cabin boy's tone was somber. "Ain't no more."

Frieda's scream pierced through Annie. She looked deeply into the boy's eyes. Joseph—the one she'd played marbles with yesterday. And the baby. What if it were Seamus and Norah?

"Wait!" Annie struggled with the strings holding the vest together. Each second counted, yet her fingers fumbled. The boy needed a vest, and this was the only one.

"Stop!" The man who held her aloft shook her hard. "What are you doing?"

The stern of the steamer tilted deeper into the water. Passengers stumbled. Some fell. The man holding Annie slammed against the railing. Her feet dangled over it, her body swaying. The contents of her stomach crested and sank with each wave that battered the ship. Still, she tore at the fastenings.

"Give it to him." Annie pointed to Joseph. "He and the baby can take my place. They don't weigh as much as I do."

"Hurry!" The man set her on her feet and snatched at her loosened vest.

The nanny pushed Joseph toward them. He stood stoically while they adjusted the vest around him, his gaze fixed on Annie.

Annie scrambled on the floor for her reticule so he wouldn't see the sobs that threatened to overwhelm her. She groped through her purse for the postcard she'd addressed to Mam and Da. She reached over and shoved it into Joseph's chubby fist. "Send it to my mam, my family," she pleaded, "and tell them…" She choked back a cry as the crew lowered Joseph into the place that would have been hers. She bent over the railing and prayed that her words would not be lost in the wind. "Give them my love."

A sailor elbowed past her and shinnied partway down the rope, baby Sarah tucked into the crook of one arm. He tossed the toddler toward waiting hands. After a woman clutched Sarah close, the sailor let go of the rope and plunged into the sea. He reappeared, head bobbing as he stroked through the waves toward a fallen mast.

Tears rained down Annie's cheeks. Mam and Da. She'd never see them again. But Mam would understand.

Frieda clutched Annie's hand as the small ship rowed out of sight. "Bless you, miss."

They remained hand in hand as the liner groaned and creaked under their feet. The stern tilted, and the ship sank deeper into the waves.

All through the night, Joseph clutched the postcard. Water splashed into the lifeboat, dissolving the edges of the thin cardboard. Whenever he awoke, Annie's sorrow-filled eyes stared at him. When he slept, he dreamed of her.

For almost two days the boat drifted on calm seas. The chilly night air bit through his damp sailor suit. People in the lifeboat huddled together in small groups for warmth and comfort, careful not to tip the boat. His lips cracked and swollen, Joseph slipped the postcard under his thigh. He cupped his hands to sip from the puddle on the floor of the lifeboat.

A woman smacked his hands, causing the precious water to dribble down the front of his shirt. "It'll kill ye, lad, for sure."

How could water kill him? Perhaps she only wanted to save it for herself. He was so thirsty. The sky and waves blended into one shimmering mass that stung his eyes and made him dizzy. Some people sprawled on the floor of the boat, others leaned back, eyes closed, their sunken eyes corpselike. Even shouts of a rescue ship barely shook Joseph from his stupor. He snatched up the postcard, toddled a few unsteady steps, and collapsed into the arms of a rescuer.

Joseph Luddington III stood beside his mother as his father's casket was lowered into the ground. Then Uncle Clyde supported his mother to the carriage, where the coachman opened the door. Heavy veiling trailed from her large black hat, hiding her face from view. When she reached for Joseph's hand, he quickly transferred the scrap of paper to his other fist. Then he clasped his mother's hand and, with a boost from the coachman, climbed onto the padded leather seat beside her.

In the trees at the edge of the cemetery, a girl stood watch, her red hair the brightest memory of that night. Joseph uncurled his hand slightly so she could see the tattered postcard before the coachman shut the door.

He was still fingering the postcard when they entered the house.

"What is that?" His mother's sharp voice startled him. "Throw away that filthy paper." She tried to snatch it from his hand, but Joseph squeezed it into his palm.

"You have no idea what kind of diseases it may carry."

Mama called for Bridget, who pried his fingers open. Bridget tossed the scrap into the fireplace. The postcard fluttered to the back of the stack of crumpled papers on the hearth.

Across the room, her body as transparent as smoke, the girl hovered over the hearth, glancing first at the scrap and then at him. Joseph squirmed. Surely she could see he'd had no choice.

After Bridget tucked him in bed, Joseph lay still, pretending to sleep. He forced his chest into a slow up-and-down motion. When Bridget retired to her room adjoining the nursery, Joseph tiptoed to the hearth and tried to spear the cardboard with the poker, but only succeeded in burying it under the ashes.

A breath on his cheek made him jump back. The girl caught the poker before it clattered onto the brick. She returned it to its place. Then she bent and scooped up the postcard. She blew the dust off it and handed it to him. He padded to his room and secreted the cardboard in his toy box. He'd made a promise that night, and he'd keep it.

That postcard was the only thing he had left from the ship. Everything else was gone. They'd forced him to leave it all behind. His toys, his dogs, his Papa.

The girl's eyes haunted him. Night after night she came to him, begging him to help her family.

Several months later, when his mother had gone to take the waters and Bridget had her half day, Joseph told the cook, who had been charged with watching him, that he would join the coachman in the stable. In one fist he clutched his pocket money, in the other, the paper he had unearthed from his toy box.

Joseph cleared his throat. He tried to imitate his father's commanding tone. "I must go to Papa's bank today. I have some business to attend to."

The coachman gave a half bow and hooked up the horses. On the way to town, Joseph sat stiff and straight beside the coachman as the horses plodded along the streets.

Again, he used Papa as an example when they pulled outside the bank. "I won't be long."

Joseph entered the bank where he had often accompanied his father, and several tellers greeted him. He went to the cage and reached up to set his pocket money on the counter.

"So sorry for your loss, son. Your Papa was a good man and is greatly missed." The teller counted the money. "Did you wish to deposit this in your account, Master Luddington?"

Tears stung Joseph's eyes as he stood on tiptoe to push the tattered cardboard across the marble shelf. "Send it to that address." Then remembering his manners, he added, "please."

The teller pursed his lips as he picked up the worn scrap. A frown creased his brow. "And shall I discard this then?" He pinched the cardboard between the tips of his fingers as if it might soil his hands.

Joseph gasped. "Oh, no. I need it."

That night the girl smiled at him, and the constant weight crushing his chest lifted. From then on, he made regular trips to the bank with his pocket money whenever Mama was away. Sometimes the girl floated along beside him when he walked, but he had to take care not to speak with her when others were watching.

If no one was around, she told him tales of her family. Her da's hearty laugh and the smoke curling from his pipe, her mam stooped over the heavy soup pot that bubbled over the fire. Her younger brothers tumbling together like a den of cubs, the older ones exhausted and blackened by coal dust. Her mam and married sisters hunched in the garden, digging up one shriveled blackened potato after another, cutting out the few useable bits to toss in the soup pot. Most nights the watery broth contained less than a handful of greens, potatoes, and meat. Sometimes only grass floated on its surface. Eight people sat down to a meal that would barely feed a small child, with little but charity cornmeal to plug the hollowness the rest of the day.

Each night as Joseph drifted off to sleep, lines of people with bloated bellies and sunken eyes, bones poking sharp angles under parchment-thin skin, empty bowls outstretched, crowded his dreams. They disappeared only on the nights he sent his pocket money to the address on the postcard.

When he turned eighteen, Joseph came into his trust fund. After leaving the lawyer's office, he booked passage on a ship sailing to County Mayo. The strange mewling his mother made when he told her reminded him of an animal in pain. Joseph almost gave in and promised to stay. But the girl appeared, staring at him with somber eyes.

"I'm going. I'm going," he assured her, waving the scrap of paper so she could see it.

His mother buried her face in a lace handkerchief, her shoulders heaving. Joseph laid one hand on Mama's shoulder and squeezed, then turned and walked away before her heart-rending sobs changed his resolve. He remained brave until he reached the gangplank.

Memories of his last walk up this slope tightened his throat so that he could barely swallow. Moisture clouded his vision as he returned to the tangled forest of trousered legs and billowing skirts of years ago. He'd clung tightly to Papa's hand, but leapt up and down to see the water. The same waves now slapping the boat made his stomach churn, his muscles tense. He stumbled back a few steps, but the press of people waiting to board hemmed him in. Panic constricted his chest, making each breath painful.

And then she stood before him, trembling. He reached out and drew her toward him. He clasped her cold hand in his own sweaty one while they boarded and then led her to his cabin. People around him shrank back, whispered behind his back as he passed. But he cared nothing for their opinions.

In the cabin, they huddled together on the edge of the bed as the whistle blew and the ship shuddered. Once the liner steamed away from the shore, she slipped from his arms. Her outline grew fainter.

The panic that had engulfed him as the ship left the dock could not compare to the terror of losing her. "Don't go." He grabbed for her, but his hands slid through empty air. "I can't make this trip alone."

"You must." She hovered a few feet from the ground, then swooped down, and touched icy lips to his cheek. "I'll see you on the other side."

Joseph pressed his fingers to the chilled spot, trying to hold the moment in his heart. Before him, she shimmered and dissolved.

To stem the tide of loneliness and fear, during the day he wrote feverishly. Each night he stood on deck, staring out to sea, one hand caressing the side of a lifeboat, pleading for her return.

As the ship neared the coast of Ireland, the seas whipped up a storm. Gale-force winds snatched his breath, blew him across the deck, and pinned him to the rail. Metal pressed into his gut as waves rose higher, splashing his trousers, his coat. Frigid water soaked through the wool until it clung to his skin, setting him shivering.

The next wave slapped him in the face. It left him gasping for air, a coating of brine on his tongue. Afraid to let go lest he slide across the deck into the sea, Joseph clenched the rail as the boat rose on the swells, then slammed into the troughs. Water poured over the sides, dragging him with its relentless pull. He came up spluttering after each onslaught, clinging to the rail. Then an anvil of water hammered against his chest, engulfing him. A white flash exploded around him. Water gurgled into his lungs, and he lost his grip on the rail. A dark liquid tunnel sucked him into the depths of the sea.

Annie came to him then, hands outstretched to greet him.

Three weeks later a trunk arrived in County Mayo. Inside a tattered scrap of cardboard bore the cottage's address. Under that lay stacks of paper. The scribbled story of Annie and the two lives she'd saved so long ago. Below that, tied in oilcloth, a will signed by Joseph Luddington III, leaving his entire trust fund to the family of Annie O'Brien.

On the hillside above that village now stands a carved marble statue of two angels, hands entwined, facing out to sea.

SURVIVOR BARBIE

BY
C.A. MASTERSON

It wasn't enough that PR spread the word that she and Ken were Splitsville. Not that they had ever been married, though God knows she'd played the bride bit about three kazillion times. All part of the image makeover, to be the girl/woman every female could identify with, aspire to be like. (As if! Could anyone on the planet have her measurements without extensive surgical modification?) But this – this was going too far. Over the edge, even! Considering she was a girl who had her own shoe store, was never far from a frilly four-poster bed, whose closet was bigger than some apartments in Queens – well, how did they expect her to pull this off? I mean, really. Barbie? On *Survivor*?

Oh well. Like everything else, she'd keep a smile on her perky face (did she have a choice?) and jump in, upturned-nose-first. Wasn't that her credo? Enthusiasm every day? A can-do attitude in any given situation? She was Barbie, after all. And Barbie might not be the newest toy on the shelf, but she was no quitter.

"Bring it on!" she told the PR guys, and packed her light blue sneakers, her pink sneakers, and some basic pink pumps (you can't go anywhere without them!) in her trunk, with 15 color-coordinated sets of shorts and tops, plus her safari hat. Oh, and she thought she better take along her yellow slicker and matching galoshes and rain hat. Just in case.

With the space she saved in not having to pack any sunscreen or bug spray (one of the perks of having been plasticized), she figured she'd have room for maybe an extra pair of tennis shoes, a couple of cute nighties, and, of course, bikinis. Itsy-bitsy teeny-weenie ones, yes, even

24

polka dot. She had the perfect bod. There was no reason not to show it off, was there?

She decided to throw in her exercise shorts and running-bra top, along with her matching wrist bands – she didn't need to work out, but she'd look really good running along the beach at sunset, her legs stretching longer than the horizon.

What she didn't guess at was that she was not to be unique among the competitors, not the only one whose face was stamped indelibly on her vinyl head, who had no use for toiletries because she never sweats. When she landed on the island, she was stunned when greeted on the white sands by none other than the dolls in the Barbie line – Teresa, Midge, Christie, Alan, Kayla, Steven, and – Ken! The producers thought their recent split would create compelling tension for the audience.

"Surprise!" they all yelled, and it certainly was. (Barbie was always being surprised; she had the attention span of a gnat.)

"What are you doing here?" Barbie was not clear – maybe they'd just come to see her off, wish her luck? But she didn't see any balloons or party hats.

"We're all on *Survivor*! Won't this be fun?" Midge squealed. But her voice hinted at some other kind of fun, the kind that usually ended with someone's feelings hurt.

As the sand beneath her shifted, Barbie tried to forget that Midge had been the first to try to steal her toy thunder. Manufactured to be a best friend to Barbie, she'd taken liberties in an introductory marketing campaign in which Barbie was placed behind her in ads, even on store shelves. Barbie had quashed that like a bad rumor.

Alan twirled a beach ball. "They said it would 'level the playing field,' whatever that means. I say we get started with a game of beach volleyball!"

Kayla and Christie clapped and giggled. "Okay!"

Steven stepped up. "No, I think we have to do these tests first, like the script says." He turned toward the cameraman. "Isn't that right?" He walked too close to the lens; on screen, the blurred flowers of his Hawaiian shirt obstructing the others from view. The producer waved him away, his face angry.

25

"Okay, okay! I'll ask this other guy." He walked behind the lighting and sound equipment where the camera could not follow. After hushed, terse instructions from someone on set, he rejoined the group, saying, "Sorry! I was just checking!"

Ken kicked at the sand dejectedly.

Barbie marched toward him.

"Hi, Barbie. It's good to see you."

"You, too, Ken. You look great."

He looked away. "That's how they made me."

After a moment of awkward silence, Barbie said, "I'm sorry we have to compete against each other. I intend to do my best, and play fair. Before we get started, I want to say good luck." She turned to the group. "To everyone! May the best Barbie win! Uh – you know what I mean."

"Yeah, we know," Midge said in a voice that snarled on her lips so her smile nearly twisted out of shape.

Barbie ignored her. "Well! I'd better get settled in! Where do we sleep?"

Vinyl heads turned toward one another. Steven asked, "Didn't they brief you at all, Barbie?"

"Sure, they gave me some papers on the airplane. But the clouds outside my window were just like cotton balls! So fluffy and pretty! Then I started to read, but I fell asleep after the first page."

Midge snickered.

Theresa said, "This isn't like a resort, Barbie."

Barbie turned her wide blue eyes inland, where palm trees swayed in the breeze, seagulls glided above their heads.

"It sure looks like one! Except there's no hotel."

Christie said, "We have to set up our own shelters. It's all part of the competition."

"Shelters? Okay, then – I'll help you set up yours, then you can help me."

"No, Barbie," said Theresa. "We can't work together as a team. The whole point is for us to do things on our own."

"Gosh, that's no fun!"

"No, gosh, it isn't," Midge echoed.

"I wish I'd brought my Winnebago. That has such a nice bed, and a dinette, and even a pool!"

Ken held up one unbending arm. "Tomorrow night, we'll have a meeting to decide who'll be voted off the island."

"People have to leave?" Barbie was incredulous.

"By the group's decision," Steven said.

Barbie wasn't liking any of this, but didn't want to discourage anyone.

In the morning, the group had their first competition – climbing the jagged rock face of a cliff. One by one they attempted to scale it, and one by one they fell. Barbie found it tough, but the unnatural slant of her feet allowed her to wedge into crevices where the men's feet wouldn't go. She managed to climb the highest of anyone, but just as she triumphantly reached toward the top, there was a zipping, a whir of rope through metal. Her harness disengaged, and she tumbled into the rocks below. A wave of mumbled concern was broken by snickering. Barbie's hand rose unsteadily from the rocks, and she dragged herself up. Her bendable legs were bizarrely splayed, so she banged her calves back into alignment. Barbie's indomitable spirit triumphed, despite the dent in her back.

At tribal council, she was saddened when Kayla and Alan were voted off the island. This endeared her to the crew, and to the audience in TV land.

In the next competition, each had to walk across a crude rope bridge before the fire burned through, sending them into the flames. Others slipped but grabbed the handrail ropes to keep from falling into the fire. Barbie went last. An ember rose and landed in the middle of the single rope that comprised the footbridge. She hurried, but just as she passed over it, the bottom rope snapped in two. She held onto the handrail ropes, shimmied along until one fell, as if untied. Barbie swung to the remaining rope, and, hanging upside down, she inched toward the finish line. The ends of her hair singed black against the flames. After falling to the ground on the other side, she patted the embers out. The crew cheered. She waved at the camera, her eyes bright, smile unwavering, smoke curling from her hair.

Barbie protested at the next tribal council when Steven and Christie were given a ticket back to the mainland. This gained her even greater support. The network execs were ecstatic that the ratings had gone through the thatched roof.

Next came the rafting competition, through Class 5 whitewater – the roughest of all – in inflatable boats. Barbie giggled as her raft slid down the jagged river. Ken used his paddle to steer clear of rocks, and swooshed past her. Barbie dug her oars into the water, too, but the boat's sides were leaking air and she was soon sitting on a sheet of plastic with nothing to hold it afloat. Midge floated by just as Barbie was knocked off the deflated raft by a rush of water. She was pushed downstream by whitewater, past the safety rope where the others had put in, and over falls that made Niagara look like a trickle. The production crew held its collective breath, watching for a sign of her singed yellow-blond hair through the mists below. On shore, the others leaned forward, strained to see.

"I'm okay!" her tiny, far-off voice echoed. Then there she was, afloat as if out for an afternoon of sun and fun. When she rejoined the group, her hair was a rat's nest. Midge offered to fix it, and chopped most of it off. She told Barbie she looked like a punk rocker. Barbie wished she could cry, just this once. In a wobbly voice she thanked Midge, stumbled to her shelter to lie down, and stared at the palm leaf ceiling. (What else could she do? She had no eyelids, after all.)

At the final tribal council, Ken and Theresa got the boot. Barbie gasped, said it wasn't fair.

Now only she and Midge remained.

Ken held an orchid. "This is for the winner."

Barbie and Midge's heads pivoted toward each other, then back to Ken.

"Each of you has skills necessary for survival. You each showed great endurance and determination. In the end, though, the votes were overwhelmingly for..." he slid the orchid behind Barbie's ear. "Barbie."

"What?" Midge snatched the orchid from Barbie's choppy hair. "No way! This belongs to me!" She ran beyond the firelight, and into the darkness. Barbie gasped when Midge screamed; her voice echoed eerily in the night.

"The producers figured she'd do that. They were waiting with a fishing net. Sounds like they caught her."

The screeching grew more distant, as if Midge were being hauled away.

"I hope she's all right."

Barbie's sympathy toward such a sore loser almost drew tears from the crew.

"She's fine. Here." Ken pulled a bigger, more exquisite orchid from behind his back.

"Oh, Ken! This should go to someone beautiful. Not me." Her choppy hair, dented back, still slightly off-kilter legs made Barbie feel like a toy refugee.

"You are more beautiful now than ever, Barbie. The viewers' votes prove that. You're a hero to them."

The camera zoomed in to her still-perky, if somewhat lopsided, face, then went to commercial.

She stood on the beach, looking at the island behind her. The helicopter's whirling blades urged her inside, along with her publicist. "Come on, Barbie! We have lots to talk about."

She climbed in, but part of her would stay on that island forever. She was a different Barbie, a new Barbie.

"Sales have been through the roof. There was a huge demand for a *Survivor Barbie,* so we've come up with a new line." He held up a Barbie doll – it looked like it had gone through the trash compactor. It looked like her.

"But..."

He held up a doll with choppy blond hair tipped with black. "Here's Rope Walk Barbie, and here's Rock Climb Barbie..."

Each doll looked as if some little girl's older, nasty brother had gotten hold of it. Barbie's laugh sounded borderline hysterical.

Her publicist continued. "Little girls all over the world are begging for these. Girls who never wanted Barbies before want these."

"But – why?"

"Simple. They can relate to you now. They're not perfect, and neither are you."

She looked out the window.

29

The island was a brown and green oval set in rings of deepening blue to aquamarine. It looked just as it did when she was arriving. Yet now, she'd consider it the place of her birth.

C.A. Masterson calls Pennsylvania home, but she'll always be a Jersey girl at heart. When not with her family, she's in her lair, concocting a magical brew of contemporary, historical, and fantasy/paranormal stories. Also writing as Cate Masters, look for her at catemasters.blogspot.com, and in far-flung corners of the web.

A SOLDIER'S GIFT

BY
DON HELIN

"They killed him. Damn it, they killed him."

Dan's daughter stood in the muted light outside his study door, back rigid, her black T-shirt telegraphing the message, "War Sucks." Dan walked over and tried to put his arms around her shoulders to comfort her. "Tina..."

She pushed back from him. "Don't, Dad, just don't. You men think you've got to be big-time warriors. See what it got him? Do you?" Tina gritted her teeth and exhaled, her eyes puffy and red. "He wanted to be an all-state quarterback just like you, then a chopper pilot just like you. So he went off to war just like you. Look what it got him. Damn all you men. And damn war."

Dan sagged back against the door as she ran down the hall, crying, her pain etched in his brain. He sank onto the red Chesterfield couch, the one Dan and his wife had bought the year before Brian was born. He placed his finger on the right arm where an eight-year-old Brian had burned a hole experimenting with lighting a cigarette. Brian had wanted to be like his dad even then.

He stood and paced around the study in his navy blue suit, heart heavy, tossing a football in the air, catching it, gripping it, and pulling it to his chest. After he walked about ten steps, he turned back and started again.

Dan stopped and stared at a picture on the wall, struggling to breathe, as if an evil force had sucked all of the oxygen out of the room.

Twenty years. Twenty years since the boy in that picture had been little. Dan had been Brian's T-ball coach, Boy Scout leader and peewee football coach. He remembered the week-long canoe sojourns, particularly the one when Brian tipped over the canoe, trying to catch that fish. How the two of them had laughed. The memory made him laugh, then the laugh caught in his throat, gagging him.

Dan's mind still couldn't compute the words from the soldiers who had come to their door. He stumbled to the window, choking, as he opened it and drew in the dry morning air. The branches of the maple tree swaying in the brisk October wind scratched at the edge of the shutter. A cardinal sat on one of the limbs, singing, but Dan looked away.

He straightened and glanced around the study, familiar but now surreal – the executive desk with its worn armchair, his first purchase, and the computer he'd finally mastered with Brian's help. How long it had taken him, and how much fun the two of them had. Yes, the two of them. Always the two of them.

Dan grabbed the football, straightened his suit and tie, and wandered upstairs to Brian's room. He stood in the doorway—the walls were decorated with memorabilia of a successful high school career: homecoming king, student council treasurer, high school diploma, and six letters, three in football and three in track.

He walked over to the dresser, and placed the football in the holder. He winced as he saw the two footballs, side by side—Brian's idea. Dan had been presented the game ball when Washburn High School won the Minneapolis District Five title. Twenty-four years later, Brian had been given the game ball when Washington Lee won the Northern Virginia regional title.

Picking up Brian's football, Dan cradled it in his arms— held it to his chest, stroked it with his fingers. Felt the smoothness. He could still smell the locker room, hear the laughter, feel the pull of the tape, imagine the pain so bad that he couldn't even raise his arms above his head, yet, then, the sweet rush of victory and celebration. God, he'd loved it, and Brian had too.

Tears blurring his vision, he grabbed the football and rushed from the room, banging his shoulder on the door frame as he stumbled out into the hall.

Dan wandered toward the master bedroom and pushed the door open. His wife stood by the window, her arms wrapped around her chest. He walked over and placed his left hand on Sara's shoulder. Began to massage her neck.

Outside the window, the wind whistled through the trees, their leaves colored bright red, orange, and yellow.

"His favorite time of year," Dan said. "He loved the sugar maples."

"I know." A tiny smile lit Sara's face. "When Brian saw leaves he thought of swirling color and foliage. You and Tina always think of raking and bagging. How can we all be so different, yet so much the same?"

"Funny, isn't it? Hard to believe that Tina and Brian came from the same gene pool." He peered over her shoulder. "What's that?"

She held up a brown teddy bear, the one with a torn ear and missing button eye. Brian's favorite.

Dan's heart lurched. "Where did you find that?"

"I kept it all these years." Sara rolled a white tissue in her hand. "I wanted to surprise him when he had children... Let them know what their father had slept with until he was almost seven years old. He would have pretended to be upset, but I know he would have loved it."

Dan nodded, unable to respond. Oh, it hurt. Grandchildren.

"Keep massaging, it feels good." She sat down in the rocker while he stroked her red hair, now tinged with threads of gray. She looked up at him. "I haven't seen Tina yet this morning. Is she ready for the memorial service?"

"She was in my study a few minutes ago. Mad. Mad at me. Mad at men."

"I know. This is a repeat of my nightmare when you were in Iraq. You were so excited to go off to that stupid war."

"And you stayed back here and joined the protests in the streets." He plopped the football into her arms, but it fell to the floor.

She jumped up and faced him. "Don't go making light of the anti-war protests." She picked up the football and kicked it, sending it sailing into a table, nearly breaking a vase. "Maybe if we'd been better at it, we wouldn't be in that God-awful Afghanistan and Brian would be here..." She slumped down in the chair, wrapping the teddy bear in her arms. She bent her head to lay her cheek against it. Cuddling it.

Dan pulled out a memory. Iraq. The first Gulf war. He'd been a young, fire-breathing chopper pilot; a warrant officer with the world by the tail. Sara hadn't wanted him to volunteer for overseas duty, but he needed to see if he had it in him to face danger and come out alive.

He flew medevac missions with a dustoff unit. As the year progressed, he found himself developing confidence evacuating wounded soldiers. Soon he was headed home, a chapter closing. At least he thought the chapter had closed, but like many of his buddies, he woke up screaming with nightmares for months after his return.

Brian had wanted to test himself the same way. How could Dan argue? Oh, why didn't he? Why?

"I can't believe it." Her voice shook him back to the present. She gazed out the window, hugging the bear as if it would run away. "It's like a bad dream. I want to wake up, but I can't."

Dan stared at her back, his face like glass, about to break. If only he hadn't told Brian all those war stories, how they'd helped him to grow.

Sarah turned and saw his face, stood and tried to take him in her arms. Hug him tight. "It's not your fault. We're going to get through this together."

Dan pulled away and staggered out of the room, then found himself back in his study, looking out the window at the leaves shifting in the breeze. Brian should be here, in his second year at William and Mary.

Dan leaned his head against the window. He had to be strong for his family, but he wasn't. Brian had volunteered for the army, gone to flight school, was flying that chopper because of him. He kicked at the floor and groaned. Too late to take all those stories back. Too late.

He collapsed back in the chair, face in his hands. Startled, he jumped up. Something in the seat. He looked down to see Brian's football lying there.

Dan stared at the ball. "How the hell did that get there? I left it upstairs." He picked it up and whirled to look around the room. Empty.

Turning back toward the window, Dan saw a little boy waving to him from out in the yard. Brian?

He pushed the window open to call out to the boy, but one quick wave and the image was gone. Nothing in the yard except the dry leaves, swirling in the October wind.

Dan stood silent, then he turned to go find Sara and Tina. They needed him. He needed them. Together.

During Don Helin's time in the military, he spent seven years in the Pentagon. Those assignments provide the background for his thrillers. Don's novel, Thy Kingdom Come, *was published in March 2009. His latest thriller,* Devil's Den *is due out this fall. For more information go to his website www.donhelin.com.*

OPERATION PUMPKIN PATCH

BY
GINA NAPOLI

Raymie, Brett, and Dosey Doe had to tiptoe home from school each day for two whole weeks. Through the woods they pranced on two hind legs instead of their usual four hooves. Lumbering Woods was too thick for them to run and play, Dad had explained. Too thick for the Doe Brothers to butt heads the way they always did in Mr. Spotter's gym class. Too thick with crunchy leaves and noisy pine needles. And much too thick with hunters.

If the hunters heard them, it meant they would be cooking deer-burgers on the campfire, their Dad had told them Monday morning. *Hunters were much worse than that time Farmer Fields shot at you when you cut through his pumpkin patch,* Dad promised.

Raymie, Dosey, and Brett begged and pleaded, but their Mom wouldn't let them skip school. The boys found their white shirts, green ties, and plaid pants hanging in their closets just where Mom always hung them. *You must do your best to keep normal lives no matter what,* Mom had said.

Walking to school, the Doe Brothers crept along the main Lumbering Woods path, quiet as chipmunks. They sneaked their way over branches, under fir trees, and through berry brambles. Dosey stopped to nibble on one, but Raymie smacked his snout away.

"You already ate the wall out of my bedroom last night, and you're still hungry?" Raymie shouted in a whisper.

"I haven't had but one apple all day." Dosey kept chewing.

"Ssh. Stop fighting. You'll get us shot," Brett said.

A horrible sucking noise sounded overhead, like a leaf-blower.

"Uh-oh," Dosey said, looking up.

Way up in a tree, high in the pine, they saw a platform attached to the tree's trunk. On the platform sat a bright orange lump with a moustache peeking out near the top.

Brett's eyelids rose. "What is that?"

The orange mound let out a huge noise, a cross between a grunt and a cough.

"Is that lumpy orange thing snoring?" Raymie tiptoed over, as close as he dared. "He sounds like Uncle Buck after a lodge meeting." He waved his hoof above his antlers, signaling for Brett and Dosey to follow.

"Or Aunt Lottie at the Thatchers' Guild," Brett said.

The boys huddled, staring at the lump.

"Do you think it's an animal?" Dosey asked.

"Nah, looks more like a pumpkin," Brett said.

Raymie waved his hooves in the air. "Are you two on salt? That's a hunter."

"A hunter?" Brett and Dosey yelled.

"Ssh!" Raymie clamped his front hooves over his brothers' snouts.

Rustling noises came from the hunter sleeping on a platform. He rolled over. The snoring became louder.

"Wait a minute," Dosey said. "Why do we have to be so quiet if he's sound asleep?"

"Don't you remember what Dad said?" Raymie said. "Where there's one hunter, there are usually more."

"And their guns, too," Brett said. "That's what Uncle Buck told me."

Dosey looked around. "Oh, I forgot about that."

"Ssh!" Raymie smacked his brothers on their snouts to quiet them, but he smacked them way harder than he meant to.

"Aarrgghh!" Dosey and Brett yelled, holding their snouts.

The hunter jolted awake. Down, down, down the tall tree his rifle fell. The rifle hit the ground and BAM, out rang a shot.

Dosey jumped into Brett's front legs. Brett jumped into Raymie's front legs. Raymie fell back into the tree.

Ka-chunk, ka-chunk, ka-chunk went the hunter's platform as it broke loose and careened down the tree trunk. It chomped down the branches like a bear eating

37

after coming out of hibernation. The cables tore off little branches as it hit the ground with a horrible thunk. Raymie, Brett, and Dosey jumped away just in time.

"What the—?" The hunter rubbed his eyes and looked right at them.

"How hard did I hit my head?" he asked himself. "Why are there a bunch of deer dressed like schoolboys?"

Dosey hid behind a log. "Agh, he's awake."

The hunter shook his head. "*Talking* deer dressed like schoolboys."

Raymie nudged both of his brothers. "Let's have some fun."

"The guys would never believe me." The hunter smacked his arms and legs, and then felt his face. "My brain musta fell out."

All three deer tiptoed toward the hunter.

"You won't be needing this, Pumpkin," Brett said as he pulled off the hunter's hat and used it to cover Dosey's spikes.

Raymie pulled a bag out of Pumpkin's pocket, holding it as far away from himself as he could get it. It was full of things that looked like pieces of tree bark that smelled like salty meat and pepper.

"Is that what I think it is?" Dosey asked.

"Probably Mrs. Mount." Raymie's voice became loud and crackly. Then he shook the bag in Pumpkin's face. "How could you make our old science teacher into jerky? She was so much better than Mr. Scat."

"Yeah," said Brett. "Mrs. Spotter let us be excused if we didn't want to dissect humans."

Pumpkin's eyes grew huge. "I have a fever. That's it." He felt his forehead. "I must be burning up."

"Let us help you cool off," Brett removed Pumpkin's coat, boots, and pants, and threw them to Dosey. "Where did you get these crazy clothes, anyway? Who would match fluorescent orange and camouflage?"

"Yeah, call the fashion ranger," Raymie said.

Dosey turned toward the hunter and clamped his suspenders between his hooves. "Mind if I take these for myself? I always wanted myself a hammock."

Brett picked up a bottle that had fallen on the ground. "Deer urine. Really? You paid $14.95 for this, Pumpkin?"

"I think we found ourselves a job we'll be good at for as soon as we graduate," Dosey said. "A real cottage industry."

"Don't shoot, and don't take me prisoner," pleaded the hunter, arms raised high above his head. "I'll leave your woods quietly."

"Take you prisoner?" Raymie laughed "Mom doesn't like it when we bring lizards home. I don't know how we would explain bringing you in the door."

"Let's dissect him," Brett said.

"Aaauuugghhh!" The hunter grabbed his boots. He looked like a frog on a pogo stick trying to put them on and lace them as he jumped away.

Dosey skipped after him, singing and chanting, "I see London. I see France. I see Pumpkin's underpants."

Brett caught the end of his coat and pulled him back.

"Those were some baggy drawers, weren't they?" Dosey asked, laughing. "How do humans keep warm with only those tiny patches of hair?"

"I couldn't get past the stains," Raymie said, making a face that looked like he had his tongue stuck to a frozen street lamp.

"Let's not think about how the stains got there," Dosey said, adjusting his new suspenders. "Let's just be glad he didn't stick with the fever theory. He would have stripped past his union suit."

Holding the hunter's jerky and his gun, Brett joined his brothers. "Now what?"

Dosey stared at his brother's hooves a long time. "Let's go home."

"Yeah," Brett said. "Meeting our first hunter could have easily gone a lot differently."

"I think we need to do something. Something big," Raymie huffed through his snout. "Or we'll be tiptoeing around for the rest of our days."

"Hunting season is only once a year," Brett said. "We won't have to tiptoe all the time."

"Nah, Brett, you're missing the point," Raymie said. "I want to show those hunters who's in charge. Lumbering

Woods is our home. They come here once a year and put fear into all our parents and our teachers. They rearrange all the dead leaves and fallen branches, and stick their stinky feet into our streams. That's our drinking water."

"They stick their bare feet in there?" Dosey clutched at his throat.

In the distance, the brothers heard "Aaauuugghhh!" followed by a splash.

"That was most definitely more than two feet flinging themselves into Cornpop Creek," Brett said. "Eeww."

"I have an idea and a plan," Raymie said, flinging the deer jerky away in disgust. "Let's call it 'Operation Pumpkin Patch.'"

Five hours later, the Doe brothers snuck past Mom and Dad's cottage, pushing past the branches and through the window cut in the thatch. First Raymie and then Brett. Dosey followed along later, meeting his brothers behind Farmer Fields's haystacks.

"Sorry I'm late," Dosey said. "Did Brett go in yet?"

Raymie clicked his hoof against his watch. "So much for synchronizing watches."

"What does that mean, exactly?" Dosey asked, leaning his wristwatch toward Raymie.

"It means your watch and my watch and Brett's watch are all supposed to match exactly." Raymie pulled Dosey's watch off and rattled it against his ear.

"Oh." Dosey pulled away. "Well, I didn't know that."

Raymie rolled his eyes. "Obviously."

"Whatever," Dosey said, peering around a haystack. "So did Brett make it to the front line?"

"Ssh, here he comes."

Whoosh! Brett whizzed past the haystack, zinging so fast that he almost smacked into the tractor.

"Oh, dear," Dosey scratched his eyelids with his hoof. "That costume's almost enough to fool me."

"Yeah, brother, you look like a real live pumpkin," Raymie said, spinning him around to show Dosey. "I do good work, if I do say so myself."

"Maybe you should quit school to become a makeup artist," Dosey said, kicking at a tractor tire.

"Don't be simple, Dosey," Raymie said.

"Aaaaanyway," Dosey pushed his way in between Raymie and Brett. His back faced Raymie, shutting him out of the conversation. "Did it work? Did you tell our story? Did they buy it?"

"As my friend Pumpkin would say, 'Yep.'" Brett laughed, taking off his bright orange coat, his camouflage hat, and his black boots. "Nothing like a campfire for making a tall tale seem believable. I couldn't believe some of their names. Jedidiah, Malachai, Marvin, Bob? I mean, really, what kind of name is 'Bob'?"

"What did they call you?" Raymie asked.

"Amos," said Brett, fishing his binoculars out of his backpack.

"This hunting gear is itchy," Dosey said, trying on the hat. "How do the woolcoats stand it? I don't see how they think they can sneak up on a deer dressed like this. This has got to weigh a ton."

"Farmer Fields's sheep don't seem to mind." Raymie swiped the hat off his brother's head and put it onto his own. Then he threw all the clothes underneath the tractor and pulled a clipboard from off the ground. Lastly, he stuffed a stub of a stick into his mouth, chomping it like a wartime general. "We're onto Phase Two of Operation Pumpkin Patch. Dosey, did you get the honey?"

"Why do you think I was late?"

Brett focused his binoculars toward the campsite. "Didn't you synchronize your watch?"

"Um, yeah," Dosey muttered, watching his own hoof poke at the hay on the ground.

"I heard that," Raymie said. "You lie like a bearskin rug."

"Ha ha, very funny." Dosey slung a bearskin rug over his shoulder and put a fluorescent orange hat on his head.

"If you thought that coat was itchy, I'll bet that rug is un-bear-able." Raymie laughed, high-fiving himself.

Brett rubbed his toes. "Where did those boots come from, anyway? They were mighty tighty."

"I borrowed them out of Farmer Fields's barn," Dosey said. "I'll give 'em back after our mission. Don't worry."

Brett lowered the binoculars. "Let's get ready. They're going into their tents."

"Shouldn't we talk in code?" Dosey asked. "Shouldn't we say something like, "The pumpkins are going into their pies?""

Raymie took Brett's binoculars and had a look for himself. "That would be a good idea if we were using our walkie-talkies, but we're standing so close we can smell each other."

"Speaking of which, I've been meaning to ask you, Dosey." Brett lowered his voice. "Did you spill that deer urine on yourself?"

"My brothers are a coupla comedians," Dosey said, pulling the bearskin over his head. "Are we ready?"

The Doe brothers formed a circle. In unison, they said, "Operation Pumpkin Patch," and clicked hooves, just like in Mr. Spotter's gym class.

Dosey Doe walked into the hunters' campsite with the bearskin over his shoulder. "Look what I found... um... Marvin."

"That you, Jedidiah? I thought you and Bill went to sleep," said Marvin.

"What kind of name is 'Bill?'" Dosey muttered to himself.

Dosey smiled when he heard a faint hum coming from the bushes.

"Yeah, I can't sleep, either," Marvin said.

"Um, well, I went walking and found this neat old bearskin. Wanna see?" Dosey backed into Marvin to let him have a look.

"That's a nice one," Marvin said, pulling on the bear's fangs.

While the faint hum grew just a little louder, Dosey stifled a giggle.

"Wait a minute here," Marvin said, pulling harder on the fangs. "What's this in the bear's mouth?"

Just then, Raymie ran through the campsite from tent to tent. "We got bear-bees! Get outta your tents! Bear-bees! Hide your skin, fellas, and run before their honey turns you!"

"Bear-bees? Honey? That's just like that story Amos told us tonight." Marvin gulped. "I thought that was just a campfire story."

I can assure you the bear-bees are quite real." Dosey turned around to look Marvin right in the eyes. "I got stung by a bear-bee, and look at me. I don't look like Jedidiah anymore. I look like a deer. Run. Save yourself."

"Sweet holy gravy!" Marvin backed away. "Bob was right about the talking animals."

"I told ya I wasn't lying," Bob clanged a tin pot with a stick. "Up, everybody, get up! We got bear-bees! Let's get outta here!"

Zippers unzipped and canvasses collapsed as the hunters struggled out of their tents. With jerking arms and legs, hunters in their underwear ran everywhere.

"This way, fellas." Marvin ran toward Farmer Fields's pumpkin patch.

Then the brothers followed behind, stopping short to hide behind Farmer Fields's tractor.

Like a swarm of bear-bees, the hunters tromped through the pumpkin patch, tripping and landing on prickly vines. "Ouch, ouch, ouch."

"Mah trapdoor keeps flying open," Bob whined. "What if the bear-bees got in there?"

"Eew, the stains," Raymie whispered to his brothers.

Just then, the porch light at Farmer Fields's house clicked on, and a shot rang out.

"I toldja to get outta my pumpkin patch." Farmer Fields fired his rifle again.

"Don't shoot, don't shoot," pleaded Marvin, still running.

"We'll never bother you again, sir," Bob said. "We're running from a hybrid breed of bear-bees."

"Ma, it's them talkin' deer again. I'm gonna get 'em once and for all." He aimed his rifle. "Hold still so's I can see ya."

Thump, thump, grunt. The hunters ran and ran. There must've been twenty sets of arms and legs flailing through the pumpkin patch, crunching through pumpkin shells and tripping through the dim moonlight. When the boys heard faint splashing sounds coming from Cornpop Creek, they sputtered their laughter into their hooves.

"I hope them dang burned hunters getcha," Farmer Fields said, pumping his fist toward the field. Then he slammed the squeaky screen door and flicked off the light.

Raymie, Brett, and Dosey tiptoed back to the campsite. Bottles, wrappers, and cigar butts lay littered around smoldering logs.

"Are the pumpkins in the pie?" Raymie's walkie-talkie crackled.

Raymie brought his walkie-talkie to his mouth. "Pumpkin pies are in the oven and baking."

Three bears poked their heads through the dense thicket behind one of the tents. The smallest bear handed Raymie the other walkie-talkie.

Brett handed a big cooler to the bears. "Thanks for your help."

"Yes, you certainly sounded like believable bear-bees," Raymie said.

"You saved our hides," Dosey said. "Literally."

And no hunters ever came to Lumbering Woods again.

Gina Napoli has published over 100 articles and stories in various print and electronic media. Her writings for children have appeared in Highlights for Children, Pockets, Humpty Dumpty, *and* Guardian Angel Kids. *Gina lives in Harrisburg with husband George, stepsons Richard and Brandon, daughter Samantha, and spoiled dog Stella.*

A CAUTIOUS LIFE

BY
LARRY C. KERR

"Did you hear about Artie?"

"No. What happened?"

"He found out his wife was having an affair."

"You're kidding!"

William Bradley listened—he couldn't avoid having the conversation inflicted upon him—as the two women babbled on in the cubicle next to his. He recognized the voice of the cubicle's occupant, Dorothy Travis, but not that of the other woman. He tried to focus on what he was doing, but found it impossible as they chattered on like a couple of magpies. William could just imagine them sitting on a wire strung between two utility poles happily squawking away and crapping on anyone beneath them.

"I swear it's true. Celeste told me this morning when we were getting coffee. She heard it from Gary who got it from Nadine. See, Nadine sits outside Artie's office and she heard him on the phone before he closed the door. She said Artie looked like he was crying," the other woman said.

"Celeste saw Artie crying?" Dorothy asked.

"No, Nadine did. It was Nadine who told Gary and he told Celeste and she whispered it to me today."

"Oh, my God. If it came from those guys it must be true."

"That's what I thought. I wouldn't have told you if I didn't think it was reliable."

William thought people should have more courtesy than to annoy him with gossip when he was trying to work. He stared at the faded gray fabric wall of the cubicle, which was high enough to block his view, but not so high as to prevent the sound of their inane talk from creeping up and over. His cube was one of many in the jungle of cubicles that filled the large room.

"Poor Artie," Dorothy said.

"It is a shame," the other woman said. "But you know he could be back on the market soon."

"Artie?"

"Yes. I know you always liked him. That's why I had to let you know."

Of course, as this conversation proved, true privacy—something he prized—was rarely achieved. That was why he took pains to protect his. When he spoke to anyone, and fortunately, his job didn't require much conversation, it was work related. After all, that's why they were there and not to make small talk. Personal business should be conducted on personal time and company business on company time. Chitchatting about family, if you had one, or the game last night was wasteful and distasteful.

"I guess he's attractive," Dorothy said.

"Come on! You had the hots for him and you know it."

"Maybe a little."

"Oh, yeah. You know it. You should walk past his office, stick your head in and say hello."

"Already? He just found out."

"You gotta put yourself out there. Let him know you're available. That way when the time does come he'll think of you first."

The plotting disgusted William almost as much as the time they were wasting. Apparently, these two had nothing else to do. He was ready to tell them to go back to work, but Dorothy's ringing phone saved him the trouble. He heard the rustle of clothing and saw a figure walk past the opening to his cubicle, although he didn't look to see who it was because he didn't care.

Happily, the gossip session was the only major annoyance of William's day. Other irritating things still occurred—he did have to answer the phone and respond to e-mails. Normally, such events would have ranked higher on his irritability scale, but after the distraction the two women caused the other things seemed trivial.

As he did at the end of every day, William followed the correct procedure for shutting off his computer and arranged items neatly on his desk. He waited, also as he did every day, for those around him to leave the office so he could exit without the bother of interacting with other people. The room was quiet when he left his cubicle and went to the elevator. However, after he pushed the lighted button to bring the elevator up to him, a man arrived.

William avoided eye contact and instead studied the digits above the entrance to the elevator and watched as the number of each floor lit up as the elevator ascended. As he waited, still another man came to the elevator.

The second man said to the first, "Hello, Artie."

"Jim," said the first man. The elevator arrived and all three got on.

It occurred to William this was the Artie the two women discussed. Since he was at the back of the elevator, William was able to observe the man. He was leaning against the side of the car, looking as though he might slide down the wall at any moment. William could not see his face, but if anyone's body language signaled defeat, this man's did. When the elevator reached the lobby he waited as Artie managed to pry himself off the wall and walk out the door. Artie shuffled along, seemingly finding the task of placing one foot in front of the other a difficult one. His head was hanging and he was looking down at the floor as he meandered out of William's sight.

That evening as he made dinner for himself and sat alone at the small table in his tidy, and blissfully quiet house, William thought about what he had heard and seen earlier. It was obvious the news of his wife's betrayal had devastated Artie. He wondered why people did it. Why did they open themselves up to such things? Couldn't they see what could happen if they trusted someone too much?

After he had climbed into bed and slid between the sheets that night, William smiled and congratulated himself for being smart enough to avoid Artie's fate. If it weren't for his intelligence, he could have found himself in such a situation.

There but for the grace of God go I, he thought before falling asleep.

William was eating his lunch, sitting in his usual seat at his usual table in his usual corner of the company cafeteria and reading a book as he usually did. He found that people did not try to talk to him if they saw him focused on his book and even if they did, he could tune them out. When he did not acknowledge them, they left him alone.

But this day was not a usual day. The cafeteria was busy and seats were difficult to find by twelve thirty. Two men sat a table close to William's table. He peered over the top of his book and looked at them, although he did not make eye contact. He didn't want to invite conversation. William didn't recognize them; he knew few of the other employees. Their faces ran together after a while, like some abstract painting.

Ordinarily, William would have ignored what they were saying, but he couldn't help listening to their conversation. Perhaps it was because they were trying to speak softly that he noticed them. His eyes flicked back and forth between his book and the two men, who were sitting catty cornered to him. He did not let his gaze linger lest they catch him or worse yet, invite him to participate.

"I don't know what to do. We've tried everything we can think of," said the man sitting farthest from William. He was perhaps forty, a plain looking man with thinning hair gray at the temples. His necktie was askew.

"Put him in rehab," said the other man, who had his back to William. He wore a white shirt and had a bald spot in the back of his head.

"It's so expensive and the insurance here only pays for part of it."

"It'll be worth it if you can get him off the stuff."

"He's been through it once. He got clean for a while then went back to his old ways."

"I didn't know that. That does make it tough."

William realized they were talking about someone on drugs. He didn't know why they chose the cafeteria to discuss it. There must be better places to talk about something so personal without involving anyone who happened to be in earshot. However, he realized some people preferred to reveal themselves to others. That was a foreign concept to him and he could never imagine himself doing it.

"We have to watch him every minute because if we don't we're afraid what might happen. We're both exhausted, and I think Mary's nearly at the end of her rope. I am, too. I keep asking myself what we did wrong with this kid."

"Don't beat yourself up. It's not your fault," bald spot said.

He knew then it must be crooked tie's son who was doing drugs. William read the same paragraph for the third time.

"I wish I could believe that. I want to believe it, but I feel so guilty. Maybe we could have done more. If we'd been better parents, he wouldn't have started taking drugs and ruined our lives."

"Unless you gave him the stuff it's not your fault. Kids do dumb things. They make mistakes and they have to face up to their mistakes."

William wondered if bald spot had been watching Dr. Phil because his counseling consisted of pop psychology platitudes. Like the TV doctor, he must think a couple of fifteen-minute lunchtime sessions would help crooked tie with his problem. With help like that, who needed enemies?

The two of them droned on and their conversation became white noise. Soon William lost interest and returned to his book. When he looked up again they were gone and almost as quickly disappeared from his thoughts.

Later at his home as William watched television, his window to the world, he recalled the conversation between the two men. Not that he was all that interested in remembering the incident, nor was he concerned about the boy's fate. He figured people did reap what they had sown and more than likely crooked tie's assessment of the situation was correct. If he had been a better parent, the kid probably would not have turned to drugs.

Lucky for him he didn't have to worry about such things because he had no children. While some people had the urge to procreate, he never had and was happy being childless. He had better things to do than amuse a child.

They were so time consuming and even more demanding of attention. He wondered if that was where the man in the cafeteria had come up short. If the man couldn't devote enough time to a child, then he shouldn't have had one. Now because of his failing there was another drain on society.

William knew he was too smart to allow himself to fall into something like that. There but for the grace of God go I, he thought as he continued flipping through the channels.

William heard someone on his porch. He parted the heavy drapes on his window enough that he could peer out with one eye and saw a woman and a child at his door. One of them rang his doorbell, but he didn't answer. He didn't know them and felt no compulsion to talk with two strangers. The doorbell rang again, but its pealing did nothing to change his mind. Someone rattled the doorknob and William tensed up, suspecting they were trying to open the door.

However, the noise only lasted a few seconds and the two of them left. William peeked out carefully so as not to move the drape and signal he was at home, and watched as they went down his sidewalk. They continued on to the next house. When he was sure they were out of sight, William cautiously opened the door, uncertain what he would find. What he did discover was a flyer.

LOST DOG
Our poodle is lost
Her name is Bitsy
If you find her please return her
REWARD

At the bottom of the flyer was a photo of the missing animal and under that was the contact information for the Edwards family, owners of Bitsy. People should be more careful with their pets and they wouldn't wander off. One of the members of the grief-stricken family had probably left the door open and the hound fled. If the Edwards' lack of responsibility was any indication, the dog could be better off on its own. Obviously, the family couldn't care for the dog. William wondered why Mr. and Mrs. Edwards had children if they couldn't even safely handle a dog.

Of course, the dog might not be blameless in the matter. There was the possibility the Edwards did care about it and it had absconded at the first opportunity. The unappreciative thing didn't know when it had life good. Here it was with a nice home with food and water and it runs off. The family would be better off if the mutt did not return.

He didn't trust animals any more than people. They were noisy, messy and had no consideration for the property of others. They chewed things. Things that weren't theirs. Then they gave the same things back, one disgusting way or the other.

Dogs were untidy eaters and had to go outside repeatedly where they made a mess of the yard. They smelled and always wanted affection. Their wagging tails were not only a nuisance, but they could be downright destructive.

Cats were another story. Although they didn't have to go outside, they were even more disgusting because they did their business inside the house. Then they had the nerve to rub against a person, leaving hairs all over him all the while making that bothersome purring noise.

Besides, he had learned through experience, pets also die. No matter how much you do for them, they perish and leave you alone. It was better to not risk getting attached to a pet than it was to lose one. Just as it was better not to allow oneself to see a woman who might cheat or to have a child who might turn out badly. It was so much better to be alone. That way no one cheated on you or turned to drugs or ran away and left you.

No, it was much safer being without a pet and thankfully he had the good sense to realize that. William glanced at the flyer once more and said to himself, there but for the grace of God, go I.

The Rev. John Bailey stood at the lectern and looked out. He'd nearly finished the service and was about to begin the twenty-third Psalm. Bible in front of him, he glanced down—though he didn't need to because he knew it by heart—-and he read:

"The Lord is my Shepherd; I shall not want.

He maketh me lie down in green pastures: He leadeth me beside the still waters."

The Rev. Bailey glanced at the man who lay not in a green pasture, but in the coffin that sat in the front of the room. He wondered about the life this man had led, for he was not familiar with him.

As a matter of fact, he didn't even know the man. The funeral home had asked him to come and speak. The Rev. Bailey was the minister of last resort. When the deceased left no instructions or if no one knew what to do with him, the funeral homes called the Rev Bailey.

"He restoreth my soul: He leadeth me in the paths of righteousness for His name's sake."

Looking out over the empty room, the Rev. Bailey asked himself what kind of man this had been. Was he such a terrible person that no one wanted to attend his funeral? He looked down at the card on the lectern. William Bradley, it said. Though the funeral director had told him the man's name, and he had the card in front of him, the name kept slipping from his thoughts. Why did he find this man so forgettable?

He'd been surprised when he received the card because there were no other names on it. Usually, the card would include the names of loved ones: a wife, a child, someone. This card didn't even have the name of a pet.

"Yea, though I walk through the valley of the shadow of death, I will fear no evil: For thou art with me; Thy rod and thy staff, they comfort me."

There was no one to comfort. However, that didn't stop the Rev. Bailey. He was here to do his job and he would do it to the best of his ability, whether or not there was an audience. Nonetheless, he found it sad that William Bradley was leaving the world alone. No one should go out this way, he thought. Surely, the man had cared for someone and someone cared for him.

"Thou preparest a table before me in the presence of mine enemies."

Did William Bradley have an enemy or was his life so insignificant that no one cared enough to even dislike him?

"Thou annointest my head with oil; My cup runneth over."

"Surely goodness and mercy shall follow me all the days of my life: and I will dwell in the house of the Lord forever."

Where would William dwell? It seemed it would not be in the heart of any living creature.

The Rev. Bailey finished the service and nodded to the funeral director, who had appeared in the rear of the room. He couldn't resist walking over to the coffin and looking at the man inside. Will my tear be the only one shed for you, William Bradley?

The funeral director and his assistants approached and the Rev. Bailey turned and walked away. He said to himself, "There but for the grace of God, go I."

Larry was born and grew up in western Pennsylvania. He was a reporter/photographer at two small newspapers prior to taking a position as a copy editor at a newspaper in south central Pennsylvania. Larry began writing in earnest in 2004. His first novel, By the Light of the Moon, *was published in March 2011.*

THE GREEN EYED MONSTER

BY
CATHERINE JORDAN

I fingered the small, circular patch behind my ear. It gave me a degree of comfort, feeling it there, although I still feared my head and stomach would recoil in spite of the patch's promise to prevent motion sickness. The second I boarded the *Queen Mary*, I had felt a degree of freedom and was anxious for the ship to sail with no second thoughts— and then I saw her. My stomach did a sudden back flip. Already I felt ill, and it wasn't the waves. On the contrary; the patch seemed to be holding its end of the bargain quite well.

Tina sauntered up the plank, drinking in the spring sun, and I knew my eyes turned even greener with envy as I compared my large waist with her bikini clad, Barbie-sized one. Really? Who the hell wears a bikini in March— in New York? And was that...? Yes, and I decided to keep my mouth shut about it. Maybe no one else would notice. A twinge of guilt hit me; a good friend would speak up right away. And we were good friends, despite my feelings, my insecurities.

I hadn't seen my friend Tina in over ten years. Like husbands and wives that had been together over many happy years, I often noticed that it was the same with friends. Some looked so much alike that they were often asked if they were sisters. Tina and I never got asked that question—other than us both having green eyes, we looked nothing alike. My fingers slid from the patch I'd been fingering to the short, tight, unkempt curls sprouting from my scalp like Medusa's snakes. Her long blond hair hung from her scalp like waves of silk. She smiled at me. Didn't look like she had changed much and I began to wonder why I had agreed to go on this trip.

We'd been roommates in college and over a recent, unexpected, long distance phone call, we agreed to vacation together to catch up on the past. Tina had always been aware of the effect she had on men. Most looked her in the eye and either turned quickly away or smiled. Some left it at that, others approached. Even from behind, men noticed her. In college, she rubbed it in my face. "Did you see that guy checking me out?" she'd ask me as we walked the campus grounds on our way to Accounting 101, or Management. I wanted to ask, "How do you know it's you they're looking at? Maybe, it's me!" However, being the smart girl that I am, I knew better than to actually believe that any of those cute guys would steal a glance in my direction, especially since I walked most of the way with my head down. The attention she received wouldn't have bothered me so much if she had just a drop of humility in her veins. I envisioned her tackling me to the ground, my face submerged in mud as she cried out, "I'm prettier than you are, and don't you forget it!"

"Hey!" she called with a wave, her flip-flops snapping underneath her. Nope, she hadn't changed a bit. I didn't expect her to be ugly. It was the hungry, conceited look in her eye that I recognized, that I had expected she would have outgrown.

I replied by raising my hand in a lazy salute, saluting goodbye to my esteem as I envisioned the two of us side by side—her in the red bikini, me in the turquoise romper. Tina, the beauty, me the beast. I think I hated her right at that moment. On the ship's deck, we embraced like long lost friends.

A tall, tan guy did a double take as he passed with a couple kids hopping along behind in his shadow. The wife, and I assumed she was his wife, trailed behind the kids. She looked Tina quickly up and down before staring right through her. Maybe she had just done with her eyes what I was doing right now—assessing Tina's man-stealing potential. In my book, the potential ranked high. But, the wife was pretty and with her wall-straight posture and slow stride, she surely had way more self-confidence than I ever would.

55

Tina smiled, tossing her long blond hair with a smooth whip of the neck, pretending to ignore all the admiration. She was loving it. I was ready to bolt. We'd spend the trip together, I knew, until she found someone to hook up with, and then she'd leave me in the cabin or on the deck. Sitting there, alone, on one of those navy blue lounge chairs. Good thing I remembered to pack a couple *Harlequins.*

"I am so happy we decided to do this," Tina exclaimed, her smile more genuine than mine. "We're going to have such a great time!" Tina squealed as she squeezed my fleshy arm. I was fairly certain that Tina's idea of a good time differed slightly from mine. It was in college. She went out to drink and hook up; I went out to people watch. I came on this vacation to relax and sight see. Tina came to see and be seen.

I returned her squeeze with an aggressive one of my own, confident that I could break a bone or two if I squeezed harder, if I really tried, if I really wanted to. The ship's horn blared, announcing departure. "Hurry!" squealed Tina. "I want to get a spot along the guardrail."

"Why?" I asked.

"So we can wave to everyone as we set sail."

We stood side-by-side, silent and thoughtful. Waving to people neither of us knew. People aboard gathered in clusters behind us, the younger ones edging against the guardrail, the older, more experienced travelers content to stand farther behind. Some chose to sit on the navy blue lounge chairs that had been pushed against the ship's wall to make room for the waving passengers. Tina occasionally peeked over her shoulder to glance at those behind, searching the crowd for possible hook-ups. She whispered, "Ah, so many men, so little time." Yeah, I'd heard her use that line many times before.

I turned to see who she might've been looking at. There were quite a few hotties. I caught a glimpse of the tan guy with the kids checking out Tina, the wife ushering her little ones closer to the guardrail, perhaps to wave good-bye to grandma and grandpa. People stared, people smiled. Eyes went to Tina's butt on display in her little red bottom.

Maybe it was the color, or maybe she really did have the perfect butt, or maybe...

Tina and I both noticed an older couple sitting close together on the lounge chairs, smiling to themselves. She elbowed me as the old man stole a quick look in her direction. Old men were always the most forward with her, quick with a compliment. His wife seemed not to notice his mild indiscretion. He whispered into her ear and she nodded, and he took a bold look at Tina's rear. Tina's mouth curved wickedly as she gave her backside a wiggle.

I giggled at Tina's provocation, mostly because I remembered what I had seen when she had first approached me. I tried to steer my attention elsewhere, aiming it toward the ones left behind on the dock. We could be those people, wishing we were aboard the luxury liner instead of actually being on it. We will have a good time, I repeated over and over inside my head.

Tina leaned seductively over the rail, hair brushing the rail. She glanced behind us once more, no doubt hoping her "possibilities" had taken notice.

"Don't look," warned Tina as she turned back to the dock, "but the old guy's wife just scolded him." I couldn't resist. When someone tells me not to look, my automatic response is elementary—I look. The old woman locked eyes on Tina's butt. What she was really looking at dawned on me. What her husband was looking at, what the tan guy and his wife had looked at, what others behind us had probably seen by now.

"Here she comes," I said. "No!" Tina whispered with a giggle, keeping her eyes straight ahead and waving. My heart skipped a beat and I turned away.

In my peripheral vision, a gnarled finger tapped Tina on the shoulder. Tina turned to face the old woman. The woman yelled over the excited hollering of vacationers around us, "Excuse me dear, but I think your tampon string is hanging down! My husband noticed it first! He wasn't sure if that's what it was, so he asked me! I thought it was a tampon string too, and knew you'd want to know!"

Tina turned as red as her bikini, then elbowed and wiggled her way through the crowd on her way to the closest bathroom, I presumed. I stayed at the guardrail, waving and hooting "Bye!" to the strangers below. Laughing, happier than I'd ever been since college, I hoped a good friend would forgive me for not speaking up.

Cathy Jordan is the author of the supernatural thriller, Do You See What I See, *to be published by Sunbury Press. A native of Mountain Top, Pennsylvania, and graduate of Pennsylvania State University, she now lives in Harrisburg with her songwriting husband and five rambunctious children.*

SMOKE

BY
LORI M. MYERS

If ever Marly needed a cigarette, it was right now, right here, inside her childhood home, filled with memories of hide-and-go seek and timeouts in the corner. Of secret kisses in the foyer. Of old chairs with pennies stuck beneath cushions. Of people in black clothing wearing sympathetic stares after her father's funeral. She was only in high school then.

"Marly!"

A raspy voice echoed from the bedroom. Marly breathed deeply, taking in the musty smell common in places where sickness had settled in for the long haul.

"Marly, is that you?"

She put her suitcase down where she stood, her gut knotting up like strained wire. She thrust her hand into her purse and heard the clink of loose change, the prick of brush bristles. Keys. Baggage claim stubs. Gum wrappers. Ever so close was her return airline ticket to home - her adopted home along the California surf - along with crumpled notepaper containing the phone number of that creepy guy in seat 36D. And then the crush of cellophane. Ah, cellophane.

She pulled the pack out of her purse and peered into it, relieved to see three cigarettes. She shook one out, and pinched the filter between trembling fingers.

"Marly!"

"Coming, Mother." *Stay light, be calm, relax. It's only temporary.*

Marly walked across the cracked linoleum to the stove and turned on one of the burners. Holding the cigarette tip to the flame, she inhaled, the warm smoke pressing against her insides and then watched the smoke curl into the air as she released it from her lungs.

"Marly! Come here."

Instinct and the past paralyzed her bones. *Stay light.* High heels and the emery board rub of pantyhose rushed at her in the form of her sister whose put-together look always took hours to get just right.

"About time you get here. And get rid of the butt!"

Marly shrugged, made a face. The smoke tasted like a first kiss. She wanted it to last, now and forever. So sweet, like a song. Stalling for time, Marly held the smoldering ash under the tap, listened to its fatal hiss, dropped the butt into the garbage disposal, then eyed it as it fell into the thick, black hole.

"You've got no common sense, Marly. With Mom sick and all from that very thing."

Ann's devotion to their mother was legendary, making her eligible for martyrdom and the owner of every sympathetic look in town. Marly, on the other hand, elicited nose-up-in-the-air stares on the rare occasion when she bothered to venture home. They're jealous, Marly reasoned, and fearful, too. Because I was the one who got away. Who couldn't be baited or fooled into rotting in a place like this.

Odd duck that she'd been as a child, she'd adopted survival tactics while growing up. Had even dressed and talked like them. Agreed with their views and politics. Followed their customs, mimicked their twang. Finally, when she was old enough and had some money saved, she'd run clear across the country, her heart beating, promising never to return. Raise her face to the California sun as the warmth melted away her scowl. Toss her shoes into the water and feel the wet sand slink around her toes. Wear men's T-shirts and bare her slim arms.

A "free spirit" her mother had called her with a disdain that Marly sensed long distance.

Marly remembered when her sister first called about their mother's illness. That had been a ten-cigarette night.

"Lung cancer," Ann had said with undertones of "I told you so." Then she'd added, "Inoperable. Stage 3B. You have to come."

Soon she'd made travel arrangements because Ann kept calling. "Mom needs you next to her one last time."

Marly had gone to the airport, hoping beyond hope that all the seats would be filled or that an earthquake would wreak havoc for at least a month, making any sort of travel impossible. When her wishes hadn't been granted, Marly boarded the flight and watched as the city lights flickered in the distance and prayed that the plane would crash. But no such luck.

Now here she was, in this place whose dreariness reminded her of a ghost town overrun with tumbleweeds and in dire need of a time machine.

"The instructions for Mom's medications are on her nightstand," Ann said. "I'll be back Sunday night. Make sure she keeps her food down. She vomits a lot."

Marly plopped herself down at the kitchen table. "Thanks for the warning."

"Stop it, Marly. I can't do everything. My nerves are shot."

"Geez, what did I say? I just got here. Don't take your aggression out on me."

"Drop the California dreamin' attitude." Ann gathered her purse and travel bag and marched to the front door. "There are harsh realities here."

"And you're one of them," Marly mumbled. She leaned back and waited for the barrage.

"Run and it'll go away, huh, Marly? If you can't see it, it doesn't exist?"

"Whatever you say."

"You're the cause, you know."

"Go on, Ann. You've been aching to say it."

"I wouldn't give you the satisfaction."

"That's nothing new."

Ann let out a puff of air. "It's all because of you."

"Because of me, what?"

Ann's eyes narrowed. "You know what I mean."

Jesus. Ann could never just say anything. What a drama queen. "I know exactly what you're thinking. So say it, damnit."

"I gave up my life!" Ann stared up at the ceiling, tears washing her cheeks, and pointed toward the bedrooms. "Now I'm left with...that."

Marly noticed the sagging beneath Ann's eyes, her
tense look, one foot cemented against the other like some
army sergeant at attention. Silence, like stifling air,
lingered as Ann caught her breath. "I just need a couple of
days away from here. Okay? Then you can go back to
your world."

Ann's voice shook; and was that a bit of gray hair at her
temple? She seemed to age right before Marly's eyes.
Suddenly, Ann turned and bolted out the door, slamming it
behind her. The rev of a car's engine and tires skating on
ice faded into the quiet night. A voice sliced through the
momentary silence.

"Marly! Come here!"

Marly shook the pack and a cigarette fell onto the table.
Two left. She had promised herself she would quit but now
wasn't the time or the place. She'd buy more tomorrow.
This town shuttered-up after sundown and the closest bar
was 25 miles away. Nothing ever changed here.

"Marly!"

Marly put the last cigarette in her pocket and lit the
other one, puffing on it like a locomotive on its last journey
and drawing on the filter until her cheeks sunk into her
face. Then she opened the window over the sink and
slapped at the smoke as it slipped through the screen and
disappeared into the freezing night.

"Marly!"

"Right there, Mom," Marly shouted between drags.

Soon the cigarette was less than a stub. She dropped
the remnant down the garbage disposal to join its mate.

Marly sat on a corner chair in her mother's bedroom for
what seemed like hours. Her mother stared at the ceiling,
wrinkled hands folded atop her comforter. A half-filled bowl
of soup and a used tea bag cluttered the nightstand under
a lamp shaded in chintz and dripping with beads. The
stink of medicine and stagnant air almost made Marly
yearn for the musty smell that had greeted her when she'd
first walked into the house. Sleet tapped like bored
fingernails against the windowpane and the radio's static
reminded Marly of the Pacific waves that had once cooled
her feet. Was that a splash she heard? The laughter of

surfers, the sound of dogs bounding along the shore, of light and air and freedom? She wanted to scream.

"Where's Ann?" her mother finally demanded.

"It's just me for a couple of days, Mom," Marly said with a hint of resentment. She hoped her mother wouldn't hear the insincerity of her words.

"You can't even take care of yourself," her mother said slowly. "Where's Ann?"

"She left," Marly shot back. "And you're stuck with me now."

Her mother turned, lips forming a sneer. "I'm better off dead than to be with you."

Marly felt the rising tension, clutched her thighs and squeezed until they hurt. "You're lucky I came!"

"Who asked you to come?" her mother snapped.

Just then the phone rang. On the other end, a male voice spoke. For the next few minutes Marly couldn't remember much of what he said. Officer-somebody. Car-something. Accident. Snow. Sleet. Do you know an Ann Westwood? Ann. Serious. Treacherous. We'll get back to you. Tell you where we're taking her.

Some sound rose in Marly's throat. Guttural. Strange. Goodbye, maybe. She hung up.

"Who was that?" Marly's mother asked.

"Nobody," Marly said. She felt fragile, like she could break. Somehow she was back in the chair. "Wrong number. Nobody."

"Whaddaya mean, nobody? What's wrong with you? Can't you even learn to ask who's calling? You never did worry about details, did you?"

Marly looked away from her mother's icy stare. Should she call somebody? Find out what's going on? Why hadn't she asked for a number?

"You can't even do something simple like find out who's on the phone."

"Shut up." Marly shook. Had she really said that?

"Where's Ann? I want Ann."

The phone rang again and Marly jumped. She picked up the receiver at mid-ring. It was the same male voice. Calling her by name this time. Asking if she was a relative of Ann Westwood.

Oh, God. She wanted that last cigarette right now.

"Yes," Marly said. "I'm her sister."

Her mother lifted her head off the pillow. Yanked the plastic tubing from her nose and face. "What?"

The male voice droned. Ms. Westwood sustained numerous serious injuries. Doctors tried their best. No sense in coming tonight. Bad storm tonight. Nothing to be done. Oh, the fetus did not survive the crash. How about other family members?

Fetus? "Just me. And our mother." *Stay light. Be light.*

Then the man said he was sorry.

Marly hung up the receiver.

"Who was that? Marly...?"

Marly sat down on the edge of the bed. Smoothed aside wisps of her mother's gray-white hair that had fallen onto her forehead. She had never bothered to really look at her mother's face before. The dimple, the lined forehead, the sculpted chin.

Her mother stared at Marly as if waiting for a sign. Then her body seemed to fold in retreat. "I'd die for a cigarette," her mother said softly.

"I know, Mom."

"No, I mean it. I need one so bad."

Marly's fingertips traced the blue veins of her mother's temple. The creases around her mother's teary eyes. She outlined her mother's mouth, thin at the top, fuller at the bottom. Much like her own. Her mother's lips quivered beneath her touch.

"You're such a good daughter," her mother whispered. "One cigarette. Just one."

Marly turned down the valve on the machine. She slipped the cigarette from her pocket and turned away to light it, taking a long, slow drag. She held her breath for a moment, then turned and faced her mother whose expression was now one of pleading, pain and acceptance. Carefully, tenderly, Marly pressed her mouth against her mother's. Together, they opened their lips and the sweet fumes swelled, exhaled from one, inhaled by another. Marly thought it felt like the pull of the ocean at high tide. Oh, how she would miss that.

Lori M. Myers is a Pushcart Prize nominee and an award-winning writer of creative nonfiction, fiction, essays, and plays. Her work has been published in national magazines and literary publications, and her plays and musicals have been performed on five regional stages. She teaches writing at York College and Penn State York, and is a reviewer/judge for the new Chautauqua Prize, a national award for fiction and literary/narrative nonfiction. Lori holds a MA in creative writing from Wilkes University.

NUMBER 11

By
MARIA McKEE

Score one for the weatherman. Last night he'd forecasted a record-setting snowstorm and I didn't believe him. This morning thick snow is falling. I haven't been to the grocery store in a week, and I'm out of all the essentials. The thought of maneuvering around panicked shoppers isn't appealing, and I'm tempted to stay home, but an empty refrigerator seems a worse choice.

By the time I reach the store, the parking lot is packed. I hurry to get bread, milk and eggs, then head to the deli. The line isn't long, but only one clerk is on duty—"Doug," according to his black and white nametag. He calls out, "number 10, please."

A woman standing in front of the deli case draws my interest. Her short brown hair is straight and unkempt. Two child's yellow barrettes, in the shape of ducks, are clipped on top of her head, but fail to keep hair out of her eyes. The nap on her coat is flat, meager, and the fur collar is ragged and patchy, as if someone took scissors to it, then had a change of mind. In one hand she grips a grocery basket and a small black change purse with a red rubber band wrapped around it; with the other, she holds up her customer ticket, number 11, as if she's at an auction.

Doug glances at it briefly. "Yes, Number 11, what can I get you?"

She points at the deli case. "One pound of this Becker's bologna."

"How would you like it sliced?"

"Medium."

Doug adjusts the slicer and cuts a piece.

"How's this?"

Eleven shakes her head. "Too thick."

66

Doug goes back to the slicer and tries again. "How about this?"

"Still too thick. Like this." She pinches her thumb and first finger together.

Poor Doug, I think. How can he measure that?

He readjusts the slicer and holds up bologna so thin, his green shirt is visible through it.

"Ma'am?"

"Too thin," she says.

Someone behind me coughs, a polite, disingenuous cough that's meant to remind the woman she's not the only customer.

Doug says nothing. He gives the slicer's thickness gauge another infinitesimal turn. "Okay?"

"Yes. Make sure you don't put those wrong pieces in my order." Her voice is a thin, flat line.

"No ma'am. Anything else?"

"One pound of this smoked turkey."

"What brand is it?" Doug asks.

Eleven shrugs. "How should I know? The tag's fallen down."

Doug comes around the counter and tries to open the deli case, but 11 is standing in the way. She doesn't move until he says, "Excuse me."

Another customer and I lock eyes in a mutual silent question: *What is it with this lady?*

"It's the store brand," Doug says, replacing the label. "How much do you want?"

"No, I don't want that crap. I want Becker's. One pound."

"I'm not sure we have it, the Becker's." He closes the lid, looks around, then sighs. Customers are rocking on their heels, staring up at the ceiling, or glaring at him, each a portrait of strained patience. He looks at the woman again.

Number 11 puts the basket in the crook of her arm and pulls a store flyer from a coat pocket. She unfolds it and shows him the deli advertisement.

Doug darts back and forth, searching the deli case. When he straightens up, he tells her, "We're out of it. I'll have to go to the back—" He doesn't say it like a statement, he says it with a question in his voice, the inflection an unspoken plea for latitude, with hope she will choose something else.

Eleven's silence is palpable.

"I'll be right back." He smiles. I think he's relieved to get away for a few minutes.

Shoppers scurry around the aisled maze of the store. Some don't have a shopping list and give the impression of indiscriminately dumping anything into their carts. Evidently I wasn't the only one who didn't believe the weatherman.

The loudspeaker blares. "There's a green Dodge pickup, license number 18D745, in the east parking lot with its lights on." The announcer repeats the information.

I check my watch. Ten minutes have passed since Doug left. A few customers walk away. I count ten others milling about, complaining to each other. "*Where's* the clerk?" someone asks. "Did he have to go to the Becker's plant for that smoked turkey?"

Somewhere in the store a baby is screaming, and I appoint that child the spokesperson for all of us.

Number 11 shakes her head and puts her basket on the floor.

Then I notice her legs and feet. She's not wearing hose or socks, and her sneakers have holes in the toes; the sole on the left sneaker is peeling away from the canvas; a Band-Aid holds it in place.

"Oh," I say quietly. I feel a cheerless dissonance between anger at her lack of consideration and pity for the circumstances that sent her to the grocery store wearing clothes inadequate for the weather.

The woman turns suddenly and catches me staring at her feet. "What are you looking at?"

The hostility in her eyes catches me off guard. Discomfited, I look away.

Doug returns, out of breath. "I'm—I'm sorry. That was my truck in the parking lot," he explains to the group. He turns to Number 11. "Here's the Becker's you wanted. Shall I slice it the same way as the bologna?"

"You are a very *stu-pid* boy," 11 says, her emphasis of each syllable a cutting whiplash.

Doug blushes deep red.

Customers begin to murmur. A man shouts, "Lady, give the kid a break, and let's get *moving* on your order!" Someone else hollers, "A-Men!"

Number 11 slowly pivots, then takes a few steps forward, scanning the crowd. Several customers step aside.

"Think you're more entitled to service than me, do you? DO you?" She jerks her chin up, and her eyes widen.

"You wanted to call him stupid, too, for keeping you waiting—didn't you?" She points a finger accusingly, jabbing it in different directions. "I *bet* you did! Holier-than-thou hypocrites!" Her voice is metallic.

Doug tries to intervene. "*Please*, ma'am, let's get back to your order."

Eleven ignores him and fires a last salvo. "Mind your own business while I do mine." She takes her time going back to the counter.

"Please don't ask her how thick she wants it," I plead under my breath, but Doug, ever faithful to his job training, asks, "How thick?"

"Just a little. Not much."

Doug inhales deeply, slices and holds up another piece. "*Okay?*"

"Yes," she says. "Okay."

"Anything else?"

"One pound of pastrami."

Doug's whole body slumps, weary and defeated. His voice is barely audible. "What brand? How thick?"

"I don't care," eleven says, "it's for my husband."

A few people snicker.

Doug slides the pastrami package across the counter, and we watch Number 11 walk away and disappear down a side aisle.

Doug calls my number. The rest of the customers begin to laugh. They make fun of the woman and mimic her words: "I don't care. It's for my husband." They repeat this over and over; they speculate about her husband, express pity for the man whose lunchmeat is a trivial matter.

Doug's face is still flushed.

"You were very patient with her," I say, hoping to ease his embarrassment.

"I'm used to it. This weather brings out the worst in people." He hands me my lunchmeat. "Have a nice day, ma'am."

I finish the rest of my shopping and push the cart through the parking lot. More than an inch of snow has fallen, a weighted, determined snow that clings to the cart's wheels.

I'm soon on my way, glad to be headed home, anticipating hot chocolate, and just as I'm about to turn into my neighborhood, I see her: Number 11.

She's plodding along with a bag of groceries cradled in her arms. Her head is covered with a thin scarf, haloed in white. Her chin rests on her chest; the coat's collar is pulled up to her ears; her bare legs are mottled and blue.

The notion comes to me unbidden and unwelcome: *Give her a ride.* Everything in me balks, but the thought returns, and like a bullet finding its mark, it strikes my strict Catholic conscience. I drive up beside her, turn off the ignition and get out of the car.

"May I offer you a ride?"

Number 11 raises her head slowly. Her eyes are wary. Judging me. Snow slides from her head into the niche between her neck and collar. I resist the impulse to scoop it away, though she seems past caring.

I tell her, as if this will make a difference, "I was in the grocery store with you." I hesitate, then add, "At the deli. I'm headed that direction, I can give you a ride." I hope she'll decline.

"Okay," she says.

I reach for her groceries. "Let me put those in the back seat for you." The groceries are packed in a paper sack inside several plastic bags.

"Don't squash my bread," she tells me.

I rummage through my winter supply basket in the back seat and hand her gloves, knee socks and a blanket. "Here. Please, put these on."

She reaches to accept the bundle, but hesitates, then draws her hands back.

"Go ahead," I urge her. "I keep extra things in the car this time of year. Where to?"

"Dietrich's Mill Road."

"Dietrich's Mill? Did you walk to the grocery store from the mill? That's almost five miles—"

"I didn't walk."

She checks the Band-Aid on her sneaker and smoothes it down, then puts on the socks. As she wraps the blanket around her legs, she shouts suddenly. "I know what you're thinking—you and everyone else at the deli! You think I'm cruel because of that clerk, Doug. The fact is he drove me to the grocery store. Doug's my son."

"Doug's your *son?*" I don't want to believe her, but her face is blank, devoid of humor. "I wouldn't humiliate one of my children in public," I tell her.

Eleven crosses her arms and raises her eyebrows. "Now that's interesting—and how many children do you have?"

"None, but—"

She throws back her head and laughs. "That's rich. No children. Well girlie, then don't say what you will or won't do. I'm helping him. I had to learn the hard way, and he may as well too—better from me!" She snorts.

I concentrate on the road. The snow is coming in thick sheets, and the windshield wipers, even set on high speed, are inadequate for the task. I pull over and brush off the windows. The trees look like specters shrouded in gray-white cloths. I'm no sooner back in the car than the windows need to be cleared again.

As I turn onto Dietrich's Mill Road, the woman says, "There—stop there." She's pointing at a lopsided mailbox, rusted and dented, fastened to a metal pole. A barely visible lane is to the left of it.

"Here? I don't see any houses. We've come this far, I may as well take you the rest of the way." But my tone is tentative, open-ended.

Number 11 gives me a piercing glance. Her answer is matter-of-fact. "Lane's not plowed. Your car will just get stuck, and I don't want a tow truck and strangers coming to my house. I'll walk."

I remove her groceries from the backseat. When I straighten up, my gloves are on top of the folded blanket; she's still wearing the socks, and I don't ask for them.

She takes her groceries, hesitates like she's about to say something, but instead abruptly walks away.

"Bitch," I mutter to myself as I clear the windows again. Out of the corner of my eye I see Number 11 stop.

"Girlie?" Her voice is strong.

I nod, but continue to clean the windshield.

"Sometimes love isn't pretty. Remember that. It's the *best* piece of advice you'll ever get."

I start to tell her that love doesn't need to be cruel, that hearts are fragile, but a sudden gust of wind raises a dense cloud of snow. When it settles, Number 11 is gone.

Maria McKee is a reclusive Virgo. Occasionally she ventures out to the grocery store or to a shoe store. If you happen to see Maria, speak to her at your own peril. Everything you say or do is fodder for her fiction.

THE THINGS SHE CHOSE TO KEEP

BY
SUSAN PIGOTT

When her heart stopped working Callie's mother fell over to her right, clipped the corner of the old pine table with her head and collapsed in a puddle of blood mixed with the last egg she had been cracking. That was how Callie found her when she came down for breakfast, and she sensed in her surprise that her life was going to get very complicated.

The ambulance came, then left, carrying away her mother's body. Family arrived. Her mother's church friends brought salad, soup and a delicious oatmeal cake.

The funeral was lovely – normal – well-attended, flowers, favorite hymns, kind words.

Afterwards there was silence. The echo of her footsteps followed her as she walked from room to room, and the sound of running water carried throughout the house. There was no sound of doors opening or closing because she had no need to carve out private spaces in the big, open house that was now her own.

She was totally alone except for the glossy black cardboard container, about the size and shape of an ice cream carton, that held her mother's ashes.

Callie set the box on the top of the kitchen pie safe. She needed to see it, not to remind her of her mother but to remind her that she had decisions to make and that she did not have forever to make them. Wednesday night was less than three days out, and she was three hundred and sixty-two miles from where she needed to be.

Her cell phone rang early the next morning. "Where are you? You were supposed to be home last night. Rehearsals begin in three days."

"I'll be there," she said. "My mother died."

73

"I thought your mother died a long time ago," her roommate said. "You're kidding."

"No. Seriously. She had a heart attack in the kitchen Thursday morning. I was packed to leave. She was making me breakfast. The funeral was Friday. Think back. I never said she was dead. Do you ever remember me saying my mother was dead?"

Five years they had shared an apartment. What had she said during those years? Very little about her childhood or her family. When the topic came up, when family holidays rolled around, "I'm an orphan," was all she offered, her voice slamming shut the door on further conversation.

"So, do you have a living father also?"

"No. He died when I was fourteen. Really. I was not close to her, and I hated him. It was easier just to say I was an orphan."

"Are you okay? You don't sound okay."

"Yes, I'm fine, but I have things to do. Papers to sign to sell the house." She looked at the box on the pie safe. "And a few other things to take care of. I'll be there. I've got to go. I'll see you at home Wednesday late-afternoon."

"That's cutting it awfully close. You can't be late. You'll lose your position for the season."

"Don't you think I know that? I didn't plan on my mother falling down dead while she was cooking scrambled eggs. I'll be there."

She slid the phone closed, cut a large piece of oatmeal cake, and poured a glass of milk. The mist was starting to lift from the farm. It was going to be another hot South Alabama day.

Just before lunch Celeste, Callie's cousin the real estate agent, came over with two sandwiches from Subway and a satchel full of papers. "Are you sure you want to list this place so quickly?" she asked. "You could rent it for a while. Or just let someone farm the land and keep an eye on the house. It is the old family homestead after all."

"It's not my home. Hasn't been for a long time. It's just the place where I was born."

"Don't be like that. It wasn't all bad."

Callie thought back. Yes, she thought, it was pretty much all bad as far back as she could remember. It got better when her father died, but by then her mother was an accomplished drunk with no intention of sobering up and Callie was already somewhere else in her mind.

"You didn't live here. Trust me, it was all bad."

Celeste went over each form, pointing out where to sign, where to initial.

"When are you leaving?"

"First thing in the morning. I've got rehearsal at six tomorrow evening. No rehearsal, no first chair this season."

After Celeste left, Callie moved through the house choosing the things of her past that she would carry into her present. There was not much she chose to keep. A tattered photo of her grandmother as a girl in front of the now tumbled- down house across the road. An elegant green glass bowl with fluted golden edges. A wooden lapboard sized to fit over the arms of a rocking chair where she cut out "paper dolls" from a Sears Roebuck catalogue when she had the mumps. Two carnival glass goblets because they were pretty and she loved the pearlized orange of the glass. A 50's era photo of her parents, newly married, martini glasses, cigarettes, her mother's beautiful fingernails in dark polish. She put them all in a box and loaded them into the back of her Toyota.

Her mother's ashes still sat in the kitchen. "Let's go down to the creek, Mom," she said in the direction of the container. Box of ashes in one hand, cello case in the other, she walked down the dirt road to the old iron bridge. It was not easy to get from the bridge down the steep bank to the water. There had been a path once, and her family had used it often during the hot summers, her father shirtless and in shorts, her mother in capris and her bra, Callie in flowered cotton underpants. She thought about the photo she had selected. Her parents had been beautiful then and passionate about each other. Callie was both the result and the end of that passion.

It had not rained during her visit and the creek was clear as winter air. The shallow water riffled over rocks and spun a fringe of foam at its edges. As she played from Barber's *Adagio for Strings*, she closed her eyes or let them

wander along the creek bank opposite. It occurred to her
that she had never gone beyond the bridge, didn't know
what lay on the other side. She searched for the water
moccasins that had sometimes joined those summer swims
with her parents. If they were there, she did not see them.

The music over, Callie untwisted the small tie sealing
the bag of her mother's remains. "Cremains," the funeral
home owner had called them. They were not what she
expected – coarser, with a texture almost like sand, paler
than the gray ash in her fireplace, more the color of bone.
She stirred them with her index finger and scattered a
pinch on the creek bank. The ashes dissolved into the wet
earth, except for a solid bit the size of a baby tooth that
remained.

She rolled the bit between her thumb and middle finger
and for an instant remembered her mother's smile from
long ago. Callie's fifth birthday when she charmed them all
by leading a dancing parade of children and parents down
the long driveway and up the hill toward town. Summer
nights when she lay beside her on the bed, listening to the
dark sounds outside, saying nothing, just running her
hand in circles on Callie's skinny little back until they both
fell asleep. Christmas mornings and the Fourth of July.

The breath caught in her throat and stalled there while
she tried to swallow around it. "I guess not yet," she
whispered and carried the box and the cello back to the
house.

It was raining when she woke on Wednesday. She
brewed coffee, finished off a container of yogurt, then
emptied the refrigerator of all its contents and dialed back
the temperature. At six-fifty, the Toyota pulled out of the
driveway, its hatch and backseat fully loaded. She noted
the time and calculated: eight and a half hours of driving,
half, maybe an hour of stopping time. Home by four thirty,
a quick shower, rehearsal at six.

She had just enough time.

The rain did not let up, and her pace dragged. Three
hours away from her apartment she felt a menacing thump
from the rear passenger side of the car and pulled into the
first roadside rest she found. By then the tire was a black

rubber pancake. Callie leaned back against the car, drenched, crying and swearing.

"Damn, damn, damn. Not now. Shit. Not now. Shit, shit, damn, shit, shit, shit. Rats."

She walked over to the sheltered picnic tables, called for roadside assistance and waited. The minutes dragged – a quarter hour, half, forty-five minutes – while she stared up the road at each approaching vehicle, hoping to see AAA. When he finally arrived the young man was able to change the tire in almost less time than it took to retrieve it from beneath her belongings. Finished, he and Callie put her things back in the car, took care of some paperwork and said goodbye.

She was forty-five minutes up the road when she remembered the box of ashes sitting on the picnic table. She remembered carrying it from the car to the shelter while she waited. She remembered listening to the rain pounding on the roof, staring at the box, aching for the five-year old she had been and the woman whose presence had been reduced to the contents of a quart-sized container. And she very distinctly remembered walking away when the mechanic arrived and not going back.

"Oh, damn," she said, pulling onto the shoulder of the highway. It was raining hard and she sat watching the fat drops splashing off the hood of the Toyota, doing travel calculations over and over in her mind, as if recalculating often enough would somehow alter the result. Finally, with a sigh, she turned the car around and headed back.

Susan Pigott wrote her first short story in Mrs. Johnson's third grade class in Charlotte, N.C., and published it there, complete with illustrations by her best friend Millicent. We don't know what happened to Millicent, but since then Susan has been a banker, affordable housing developer, college professor, journalist, perennial wrangler and church administrator. She lives in Mechanicsburg with her husband, their cat and the black snake that overwinters in their basement storage room.

THE SURPRISE PARTY

BY
CAROL A. LAUVER

"Happy birthday Enid, you're ninety-two years old today," she said smiling to herself.

The last ten years were etched on her face like tree roots. Red had always been her favorite color. She was wearing varying shades that glowed in her hair, toenails, and fingernails. "Ravish Me Red" lipstick by Revlon adorned her mouth. Her favorite house dress had red roses on a navy background. She glanced in the mirror and saw herself still in her twenties, beautiful and vibrant. Breakfast was to be long-cooking oatmeal and hot chocolate made with cocoa powder, milk, and sugar.

Today was not only special for her, but she was planning to surprise her twin sister Ethel with a birthday party. Her husband Horace hadn't been let in on the secret because he had loose lips. After seventy-two years of marriage, he forgot a lot and wasn't helping anymore since he became ill.

"Ethel will be shocked," Enid thought. Enid pictured the look on her face: the same look Ethel had when they were five years old and their mother surprised them with a pottery glass children's tea set. The set was imported from Germany and carefully packaged in a cardboard box. On the box lid in red and blue was a picture of two girls and their dolls playing with the tea set. Inside the box were a tea pot, sugar and creamer with six cups and saucers. The most beautiful red flowers and green leaves with blue trim were painted on each piece. That was the best birthday and gift they ever had. The following year their mother died of pneumonia. Both girls were never the same after her death. They visited her graveside everyday after school to tell their mother stories about their day. The loss of her was difficult and painful. Their father never recovered from

78

her death and fell into a deep depression. He raised them
the next fourteen years with a heavy heart. One day,
without warning, he joined his wife.

Enid had caught Horace's eye at the bank one day and
he was smitten. She was tall, thin, and striking at the age
of twenty. Horace didn't waste any time in offering a
marriage proposal to Enid. She accepted with one
condition that Ethel would come and live with them in
their Victorian home. Horace had no problem with Ethel
moving in and giving his wife a hand and companionship
while he was away at work. The exterior of the house was
brick red with navy shutters and a heavy wooden door.
This was her dream house to be filled with the laughter of
children. Enid's pregnancy was a joyous time for the three
of them. Ethel was happy again, looking forward to
becoming an aunt. She felt as if she were having the baby.
Horace and Ethel were planning a surprise baby shower.
Everything was in place and then the unexpected
happened. Enid tripped on a loose floor board and fell
down a flight of stairs. Instead of a joyous time the house
was filled with tears and mourning. The still born baby was
buried next to their beloved mother. After years of trying
and the disbelief that she would never be able to conceive,
Enid finally accepted the doctor's diagnosis. Life went on.
While Horace worked, the twins stayed at home cooking,
cleaning, sewing, and organizing the church bazaar. No
matter what the weather the women continued their
childhood ritual of visiting the graves of their mother and
baby Edith.

Enid took out her notepad and listed Ethel's favorite
foods: roast beef, mashed potatoes, glazed carrots,
Brussels sprouts, and coconut cream pie. After checking
the pantry and refrigerator she needed to go out to the
garden and pick the carrots and Brussels sprouts, cook the
meat, and later clean, cut, and boil the potatoes. Once all
that was done she would make the pie. Everyone loved her
pies. For the church bazaar she would make a dozen pies.
Parishioners would line up in anticipation of buying one of
her famous pies. Enough self congratulation, she needed to
get busy. She slipped into a sweater, grabbed her red and
blue woven basket, and opened the kitchen door. The

garden supplied most of their vegetable and herbal needs. The growing season already peaked. Enid hoped there would be enough for today's dinner. The weeds scratched her bare legs as she walked through the sparse garden.

"Good," she mumbled to herself, "three carrots and ten Brussels sprouts left. This will have to do."

She felt a little dizzy bending over. It was time to take her vertigo medicine. The neighbor's gray tabby cat, Mr. Jingles, raced over for a pet. Enid loved cats and cats loved her. She wished she owned one but Horace and Ethel were allergic to them. Back in the house, she lifted out the vegetables from the basket. Later she would pick a bunch of mums, Ethel's favorite. They would look festive on the dining room table.

Enid and her sister always said, "The best part of the meal was the dessert." She set to work getting out the ingredients: half and half cream, two eggs, white sugar, all purpose flour, salt, coconut, vanilla extract, a pie shell, frozen whipped topping, a medium sauce pan, and measuring spoons and cup. The smell of the ingredients overwhelmed her senses and evoked memories of her youthful days with Horace. She had loved him so much. She missed his sense of humor and his playfulness. Now he sat in his wheelchair reading a book or newspaper. He had no need for conversation, just a nod. Ethel sat in her wheelchair looking into space. She refused to visit mother and the baby. There was nothing she could say to change Ethel's mind. The house was as quiet as a morgue. But Enid was still grateful for the company. Maybe today the celebration would spark a birthday song or conversation. She was hoping today would be different.

Enid poked her head around the corner to see if her loved ones were sitting in their usual positions. Yes, the same scene had played out for years. She asked them both if they were comfortable. Did they need a cup of tea or something to eat? No nothing they seemed to say. Okay, she would continue preparing the meal. Later a bath was in order and she would put on her favorite blue satin dress with red roses.

Enid began slicing the large yellow onion. This one was particularly hot because tears filled her eyes. If someone

walked in on her they would think this was her saddest
birthday. On the contrary she felt needed and loved and
that was all she wanted in life. She scooped the onion into
the hot oil of the Dutch oven. After the onion clarified she
added the roast that had been floured and seasoned. Enid
browned the meat on all sides, added a cup of water and
beef bouillon. Once the water boiled she would simmer the
meat. The vegetables could wait a little, next was the
dining room table.

The beautiful oak table and chairs were a gift from her
father when she married. It had served her well over the
years. She took out the red table cloth and pressed the
wrinkles away with her hand. Next the blue dishes were
taken out of the china cupboard and arranged on the table.
Everyone had their favorite place at the table. Horace sat at
the head of the table. Enid sat to the right of Horace and
Ethel to the left of him. The heavy chairs had been moved
away from the table, wheelchairs were used instead.
Silverware, napkins, and glasses would be taken out of
their resting places and arranged accordingly.

Enid was exhausted. She had been preparing for this
dinner all morning. Before she lay down she checked on
the roast. It needed another cup of water. It smelled
delicious and Enid's stomach growled with anticipation.
She couldn't do another task until she took a nap. The bed
was unmade and she crawled in, setting the alarm for one
hour. Sleep enveloped her body and she dreamed of
happier times.

Enid and Ethel were five again celebrating their
birthday with mother and papa. Their mother had sewn
matching red dresses for her and the girls for this special
day. The girls wore blue hair ribbons in their long chestnut
colored hair. The four of them were sitting at the twins'
play table surrounded by porcelain dolls and using the tea
set they had been given. The imaginary tea was the best
they had ever tasted and the dolls agreed. Everyone was
laughing and having a wonderful time. The twins were
singing "Happy Birthday" and serving cake. It was the best
birthday that anyone could imagine.

Enid had a smile frozen on her face when the firemen
found her dead from smoke inhalation. The roast that she

had carefully prepared with so much love had cooked down and burned in the pot. The paramedics were unable to revive her. A small article appeared in the *Briartown Gazette* the next day: "Elderly Woman Found Dead with Two Embalmed Corpses. It appears that Mrs. Enid Mayfield, 92 years old and a lifelong resident of Briartown could not bear to live without her husband Horace and her twin sister Ethel Frankel. Evidently Enid had removed the deceased after their funerals and kept them at home for the past decade. The two corpses were seated in the living room in wheel chairs with newspapers in their laps. The dining table was set for the evening meal."

Carol Lauver attributes her love of the arts from living in New York City during her formative years. She studied ballet at the Metropolitan Ballet Co., visited the world famous art museums and attended concerts. She loves to do experimental art, write, read, cook and occasionally act. Her vocation is teaching kindergarten. She is married and has one son, two cats and one parakeet.

AN EXCERPT FROM
"OOPS," SAID GOD

BY
DUFFY BATZER

God stood with his hands clasped behind his back, watching the scene playing across his office window. He gave a long sigh and the image disappeared. God closed his eyes briefly then opened them, trying to let the beautiful visage of clouds and sky that had replaced the violent escapades calm his nerves. His shoulders slumped. It hadn't worked. Rubbing his temples he said out loud, "Peter, could you please send Adam and Eve along with Lassie the First to my office, please?"

"Of course, sir," Peter's efficient voice replied.

For the hundredth googolplex time, God wondered why he had created humans. He knew it made him Infinity's joke, but really. No one had bothered to explain independent thought and free will to him. God had been in the middle of a correspondence course in Deitism and had really only created Adam and Eve as a model for what he was reading. It wasn't his fault if, while he took a nap between cramming sessions, they had gone and eaten a node from one of the Earth's computer antennas. He had never even fathomed that they might find it edible. Another lesson he had apparently not reached in his course: sentient beings will try anything once.

So God was stuck with the Earth and the damned smart yet determined-to-be-ignorant Homo Sapiens. He had tried to make things better. He had bent the rules and tweaked history a little and inserted an enthusiastic carpenter to try and explain to everyone how much better the world would be if everyone lightened up and loved each other more. The death toll from that had been so large that the Central Omniscient Being Council police force had come along asking questions about his intentions for this

83

small planet. They had threatened an audit of his galactic taxes to make sure he wasn't trying to somehow use this planet for fraud. Therefore he had to content himself with just keeping things on track until the end of what his humans called "time." It was their problem if they wanted to make that time as miserable as possible.

I should have stopped when I created the dog, God thought, not for the first time.

As these thoughts ran through God's head, Adam and Eve and Lassie were in an elevator on their way to his office, as ordered. Eve smoothed her skirt a bit, even though it wasn't wrinkled. There were no wrinkles in Heaven. That did not pertain to noses though, and she wrinkled hers as Adam lit a cigarette.

"Must you?" she asked Adam. Lassie thumped her agreement to Eve.

"Well, it's not like it is going to kill me, is it?" he replied through a stream of smoke. He slipped his lighter back into the inside pocket of his suit jacket. If there was one thing Adam and Eve were, it was well dressed. Lassie figured it was a subconscious reaction to running around in fig leaves for a lifetime.

Lassie felt a headache coming on. This was the usual reaction to working with humans. She rubbed up against Eve's leg, and Eve reached down and scratched behind Lassie's large, pointed eyes. That was better. They were good for some pampering at least.

The elevator door opened and the original couple looked out into God's reception lobby. The floors and wall were all clear, except the right side where there was a door and opaque brown wall, giving the occupants a spectacular view of the clouds and sky of Heaven.

Straight ahead of the elevator was a large brown lacquered desk where Peter stayed with his back to the room, looking out of the wall behind him. Lassie moved to the right and lay down in front of the door to God's office. Eve and Adam walked to the front of Peter's desk. They glanced out of the window to see what had the usually diligent Peter distracted. There was a volleyball game going on outside. In Heaven, this was always an interesting sport, as the players would play with wings attached. It made for some very exciting spikes. Adam cleared his throat. Peter jumped and turned quickly around.

"Oh, sorry about that," he said as he shuffled some papers around his desk. "This is a big game. Gabriel and I have a bet on."

"Really? Do tell," Adam said.

Peter went slightly pink and cleared his throat. "Well if the gold halos win, I do as well. Gabe's got his bet on the silvers."

"And what, pray tell, does the winner get?"

At this Peter blushed even more and cleared his throat. "The winner gets to be god."

Adam replied, "Don't we have more than enough of those around here?"

"Oh, not God, but god," Peter said in a rush. "Whoever wins gets to go down to Earth and put on the show next time some fanatic gets into an overzealous and/or drunken state. I really hope I win, because I really want to outdo Gabe's Joseph Smith performance. It's legendary."

"It should be," Eve said. "It's caused enough problems."

"Yes, well, be that as it may. . .you are, naturally, expected." And with that Peter went back to shuffling the papers on his desk.

God was still standing looking out the window when the trio entered. Adam and Eve sat down in the two chairs that were placed before the desk. Adam lounged back and put his feet up on the desk. Lassie went to God's side and licked his hand. He patted her on the head.

"It looks like Peter is going to get his chance. The golds are about to pull ahead. Mary Magdalene just joined the team, and she has a killer serve."

"Among other talents," Adam replied. Eve crossed her arms and raised her eyebrow at him. He added, "Or so I have heard, darling. Jesus will run at the mouth if you get enough tequila into him."

God cleared his throat as he turned. He coughed a touch and glowered at Adam's cigarette. "On to business." The window behind him darkened and the battle scenes God had been watching before the volleyball game had distracted him appeared again. "What you are looking at is

New York City for alternative history date April 27th, 1938."

Adam sat up and dropped his feet to the floor, leaving scuffmarks on the desk. Eve's eyes widened. "Who in the world is attacking the United States in 1938? Did something change to give the Austrian twit a head start and advantage?"

God sighed before saying, "It's Canada, all right?"

A laugh burst from Adam's lips. "How did you manage to let anything between the U.S. of A and Canada get bad enough to lead to war?"

God's eye's narrowed. "Well, it was such a round-about cause that the computer could not compute the outcome before it happened. You see, it's all about a girl."

"It always is," Eve sighed. "I am really tired of getting the blame for these things."

"Dearest, no one is blaming you," Adam comforted her. "At least no one in this room."

There was a pause. Adam looked up at God, who jumped a little and replied, "Of course not."

Eve smoothed her skirt with her hands. "Anyway, proceed."

"It all really starts at a ball in 1910," God continued, and the picture changed to a huge ballroom, then the image zoomed in on a group of young men surrounding a particular young woman. She was talking animatedly which made her elaborately styled, shiny brown curls dance. When she laughed her violet eyes twinkled.

"You are looking at Mademoiselle Annabella Dione, the belle of Montreal. Now here are the young men we are interested in." The picture zoomed in on the two young men who were the closest to Annabella, and obviously the most rapt. "The blonde is Gregory Finch. He is an up and coming American. Currently he is working on the staff of the American ambassador. Eventually he will be an adviser to Herbert Hoover. The dark haired fellow is Jonathan Goodling. He is a member of the Canadian Parliament." Eve walked closer to the screen and tilted her head as she studied the two boys. Gregory's face had an earnest, serious expression as if Miss Dione's conversation carried the weight of the world. They watched Jonathan change from laughing to smoldering rage as Annabella touched the lapel of Gregory's jacket and then to adoration and passion as her shoulder brushed his when she turned to gesture at the painting behind her.

God said, "Originally, Jonathan did not make it to the party. It all starts with a feather."

"Oh this is the part of the story I love," Adam declared as he plopped himself down in God's chair. "Let me get comfortable. So what random series of events has led to this catastrophe?"

God squinted at him, but continued. "Well it starts with Goodling's tailor. He's rather fond of the seedier side of town, mostly underground, bare-knuckled fighting. He's a big gambler. Anyway, we have to go back to a round of fights the night before he made the tux Goodling is wearing. Originally, the fights broke up early as no one would come forward to challenge the champion." The image on the wall turned to a smoke filled basement filled with sweaty and cheering men. In the middle was a human mountain with a shaved head and a face like a bull. He snorted and Adam could have sworn he saw steam leave the nostrils. He gave a long, low whistle. "I can see why. The man also looked like he hadn't bathed in a, well, ever."

"Yes, well, in the alternative, a short man with a feather in his hat walks by a taller man. The feather tickles the taller man's nose, making him sneeze. As he sneezes he stumbles into the ring, and the challenger immediately pounces." Again the scene played out in front of them. A tall, thin man was doing his best to stay out of the monster's grasp, trying to get out of the ring, but the men surrounding kept pushing him back in, shouting and laughing. Money was quickly changing hands. "Now, if only this unfortunate man had just gotten knocked out, and everyone gone home, but alas, no." For a few panicked moments, the tall thin man scrambled around, barely dodging punches, then suddenly his defense seemed to become more structured. His strategy seemed to be: don't get hit. This went on for fifteen minutes. The champion was wearing down. Slowly his punches got sloppier, and his defenses were lowering. The tall thin man threw one punch right at the champion's jaw. It was blocked with a forearm,

87

and the tall thin man took a fist in the gut. He didn't get up, though a small groan escaped his lips before he lost consciousness.

With a grimace on her face Eve said, "That was unfortunate."

"Yes," God replied. "Especially in that it set this whole sequence of events in motion. See the old man in the back that looks like he is made out of toothpicks and sandpaper?" Both Adam and Eve nodded, and Lassie gave a little affirmative woof. "That is the tailor." He was jumping up and down and giggling. "He just won a lot of money. He will spend the rest of the evening getting drunk." The picture changed to a pub and a raucous group of men surrounding the tailor who was obviously a shot away from passing out, but still had a huge grin on his withered, old face.

"This night of partying leaves him tired the next day, but he is on a deadline to finish the tuxedo for Mr. Goodling." Now the old man was sitting cross-legged in his shop, desperately trying to keep his eyes open as he put in the hem of a pant leg. He still had the grin on his face. "Right here, during this yawn, he is going to drop a stitch." Then in fast forward, a delivery boy picked up the suit and took it to the Goodling residence. They watched Jonathan Goodling meticulously prep himself for the ball; he then began to leave. "Here is where the feather, the winning bet, and the missed stitch become significant. Right before he reached the first stair, Goodling stopped and leaned down to pick at the string hanging from his cuff. As he did that, a cat came streaking across the top stair. God paused the picture and pointed at the cat, saying, "In the original time line there was no string. Goodling kept going and ended up tripping over the cat, taking a spill down the stairs and breaking a leg. Instead he ends up as we saw him at first." The wall was back to Annabella and her suitors.

Finally Adam said, "Not to spoil a perfectly good story, but why don't we just go and steal the short man's hat, or stop him or the tall thin man from going to the fights?"

God shook his head, "Somehow a change in the original code for Earth's history happened. It is very tiny, within an acceptable margin of error. A glitch, if you will. No matter

88

what scenarios I run, that fight ends up happening. One way or another the tailor ends up drunk and missing that stitch. Even sneaking into Goodling's room and cutting the thread can't work. He doesn't leave the suit from the time it arrives until he dresses, and he won't no matter what happens in the house. I even tried pushing him down the stairs or a trip wire, and it always ends worse than the broken leg. I even briefly contemplated setting a small kitchen fire, but that leads to changes well outside parameters."

"I didn't think a glitch like that was possible," Eve commented.

"Neither did I," God said in a troubled tone. "We will be working on that while you are on the ground."

"Well, they both have the look of men who would rather draw pistols at dawn than share a beer," Adam quipped as he turned from the screen back to God. "So, we are looking at the beginning of a jealousy? Which of them gets the girl and which starts a war?"

"Neither of them—and both."

God and Adam started when Eve spoke. God replied quizzically, "That's right. How did you know?"

"Because our Mdm. Dione has been doing her best to make this young waiter here jealous. She is laughing a little too loudly, and every time she touches one of her admirers, she glances at him. And he has been carrying around those canapés on his tray for an hour without serving one of them."

God sighed. "Dear Eve, you have excellent perception. If only you could have developed it before the apple. In three days, Annabella will be running away with the dashing waiter, Henri."

Adam clapped God on the shoulder. "You know you have to be thankful for one thing."

God arched an eyeball at him. "And that would be?"

"At least when the planet computer went crazy, it only spewed out a finite amount of basic human predicaments."

God folded his arms across his chest. "Yes, I suppose that is something, but they do excel at making them all tangled messes."

Lassie reached up to the screen and scratched at the feet of Gregory and Jonathan and a low whine escaped her lips.

"I agree, Lassie," Adam said nodding and giving the dog a quick scratch behind the ears. "And instead of commiserating over my suggested plethora of beers, they choose to blame each other?"

After a thoughtful pause, God replied, "Well, I suppose it is something more along the lines of hurt pride. You see, as these stories often go, Annabella's family would never approve of the waiter. To keep everyone from finding out before the elopement, Annabella is leading both men around by the nose hairs, rather publicly. Then to add to the confusion, she accepts both of their marriage proposals the evening before she and Henri make their escape. Again, this wouldn't have happened originally as Goodling was convalescing at the time. Finch was given the chance to propose and consequently was the only one spurned. Once the truth is discovered, both men are humiliated, naturally. The only target to take that humiliation out on is each other as Annabella and Henri are happily on a ship to France with all of her and most of her mother's jewels."

"Hm, you have to give the eloping couple credit for style and out and out, well, balls," Adam said. Both Lassie and Eve nodded in agreement.

"More than you may realize. Annabella and Henri will open a hotel and dance hall when they get to Paris. It will become rather well known. Come World War Two, it will be a favorite of the Nazis." Again the screen flicked. Henri and Annabella change into a middle-aged, well-dressed couple welcoming men in SS uniforms with French ladies on their arms. "However, they are also high ranking members of the French resistance. Thanks to their free flowing liquor and charisma, they become a top source of crucial information that will be used against the Nazis. Their elopement and presence in Paris is essential." The couple was shown going through the pockets and luggage of one of the officers while he was passed out on the bed, snoring. A half-clad young lady was aiding them.

"The Nazis certainly knew how to appreciate a nice set of bosoms," Adam commented.

Eve glared at him. "You know, for someone who was never a baby or breast fed, your breast obsession is rather disturbing."

"It comes from having access to the very first pair ever made, darling," Adam replied to appease her.

"So run along to Montreal, keep Misters Finch and Goodling from becoming bitter enemies while making sure the future of the object of their shared love or hatred, however you choose to look at it, is not changed."

Duffy Batzer is an on-hold teacher while she educates the two children she has to actually raise. She has wanted to be a published writer since her first grade teacher bound, Silver the Flying Unicorn, *between two pieces of wallpaper.* "Oops," Said God *will hopefully be her first novel soon...ish.*

SWAN SONG

BY
ANN ELIA STEWART

She pulled into the parking lot several paces behind the ambulance, and turned off her engine and lights. A red strobe bounced off the car's custom leather walls, her presence illuminated by jagged strokes, but to whom she could not know—no one yet had emerged from the ambulance. It simply sat with its incessant light poking through the night, hemorrhaging onto the rain-soaked asphalt, reminding her that this indeed was not a dream.

Minutes might have passed, perhaps even hours as she sat in limbo watching a set of double doors at the back of the hospital. She suspected the driver and passenger of the ambulance had been doing the same, blowing smoke out their windows, streams of poison mingling with the fog, adding to the film noir of her reality.

A woman in a long, white lab coat pushed through the back doors. Driver and passenger bolted from the ambulance, their cigarettes skipping across the asphalt like miniature orange comets. The fat one stretched, his shirt rising over his dumpling belly. He sported a shaved head, round like a pumpkin's.

The door handle was cold. She must have been sitting there for hours. Maybe one. She waited. They huddled in conference, but their conversation struck her as too jolly.

They have no idea.

The fat one with the shaved head broke away from the group and opened the ambulance doors.

Her handle gave way, yet she waited, eyes riveted to those doors. The attendants flanked a gurney carrying a shiny, black bag, the red strobe catching its sheen, reminding her, of all things, patent leather. Red patent leather shoes. Tap shoes.

She opened the car door and rushed them, water splashing into her spiked-heeled shoes.

"I need to go in with you."

Surprise animated their otherwise bored faces, people who take death, injury, profound illness in their stride, just another claim to keystroke into the system.

Lab Coat Woman spun around, her sneakered feet squeaking on the wet asphalt.

"You can't."

As if I have no right. "I'm coming inside."

Lab Coat Woman studied her, her voice softening. "Look, I know this is terribly difficult, but I'd be breaking regula-"

"Are there regulations when they're born?" She held her gaze. Woman to woman.

Lab Coat Woman broke free first, preferring to look at the ground.

Rain pooled in the creases of the black vinyl bag. She swept a small wet puddle to the ground. "It's cold. Can we please go in? I'll sit by the door, that's all. I'll just sit there."

"I know how hard this must be—"

She stiffened under Lab Coat Woman's attempt to soothe her, drawing in her fruity, sweet scent. She hated that kind of perfume, found it cloying, unnatural. "Won't you grant me this?" she heard herself say to this person who smelled like a teenager, this person so concerned with following the rules, even now. "I'm asking to sit there, outside the room. I just want to be — there." The lab coat sleeve was rough in her clutch, something real at least. "Please, I need to do this."

The sky unleashed sheets of rain, the damp, dank air penetrating to the bone.

"Okay. Come along then."

There are no shadows here. She turned her head first to one side, then the other, the white linoleum softened by a few spent florescent bulbs. Her ass hurt, the metal card table chair someone brought her felt like a marble slab.

She closed her eyes. The doughy light helped her sink into a void.

A late summer's day. The tang of freshly squeezed lemons stung her nose, the clinking of ice cubes, a daddy sawing wood for the coming winter nights to be filled with hot chocolate, pizza by the fireplace, the little girl twirling around the yard, her hands clasped together over her head, her long, blonde ponytail snapping side to side with each pirouette.

"Christina! I brought you and daddy lemonade."

She detected joy. She may be smiling.

He was smoking a cigarette, its foul tip dangling from his lips, the curl of smoke writhing through the air she breathed, those innocent lungs, that beautiful, clean little body. He promised he'd quit smoking and drinking after the baby was born. He promised a lot of things.

Her eyes snapped open. She wanted the relief of tears, she wanted to hear herself scream.

A dull buzzing pierced the stillness. Long strokes of sound came from behind the door, like a toy, a reasonable facsimile of a chainsaw.

She glanced again down the hall, the endless hall with the blazing orange EXIT sign.

She closed her eyes, the buzz making her flinch.

"Still here?"

A black blazer now draped Lab Coat Woman's slim shoulders, a pink ribbon attached to its lapel.

"What have you found?" She watched for any expression, any sign. An answer. A confirmation. To her surprise, the woman's stoicism faltered.

"I've printed a copy of the report for you."

She stared at the pink ribbon.

Christina's toe shoes, their trailing, satiny, pink ribbons wrapped around her ankles, her calves. Oh, how high she'd reach, how tall and proud she'd stand, defying Miss Anastasia's repudiation, imagine the stupidity of that woman punishing this beautiful gazelle for a gene she had no more to do with than those born short and stick thin: Miss Anastasia's idea of Odette.

Save for one — Christina's senior show, Miss Anastasia's conspicuous absence. She wanted her to stay, to watch Christina rise to her full height, Odette awaiting

her Prince, her body a perfect arc, her toes tipped as if
teetering atop a music box, accomplished and proud.

She wanted Ms. Anastasia to realize the mistake she
had made all those years, relegating Christina to chorus.
Did she ever know disappointment? The situation offered
her no choice — she had to mention the little nips Miss
Anastasia took, before, during, after practice. She had kept
silent too long. The more she nipped, the more unreasonable
she became. "Strict," the board chairman tried to label it.
"Irresponsible," she countered. "Bad role model."

Lab Coat Woman's hand warmed her own.

"We're taking the body—"

"Christina."

"Yes. We're taking Christina to the funeral home now."
She lowered her eyes and rifled through her papers.

"Is my car safe here?"

"Excuse me?"

"I wondered if my car would be safe here."

"I'm not sure what you're asking."

"I'm not asking. I'm riding with her."

Christina's fiancé wore his hair like the fat attendant's,
a shaved head revealing the bumps, the imperfections of
his skull. That purplish stain at the back of his neck.

The first thing he said, before Christina had a chance to
introduce him, was, "Smells good in here. I like a woman
who knows how to cook." Surely, he had meant it as a
compliment. And then he scooped her daughter into him
and nuzzled her neck. "She wants to show me something,"
he had said, except it came out sounding like "sump-in.'"

She stood in the kitchen watching the two of them
cross the backyard, Christina at least three inches taller,
her arm linked inside this bulldog of a person. She could
never have pictured this.

She stroked her daughter's face, pulling the zipper
further down, the bruises around her neck like a tattoo of
a Victorian collar.

Death by electrocution, the official ruling.

Indeed, soot flecked her daughter's aureoles, her
nipples encrusted with dried blood from the bite of the

clamp. It diverted her attention from the filet of Christina's torso.

A phone rang in the front cab.

She was standing in her kitchen, calming Christina, trying to make sense of this beautiful young woman repeating how she deserved to be punished, that she had been bad.

"Christina, listen to me. You tried to get free, honey. That's why you left him. You should never have gone back. Come home now, darling. Right now, just come home."

She unzipped the bag its full length, rolled her daughter to her side, so gentle.

There was blood in her urine. *I've printed a copy of the report.*

She inspected Christina's back. There, at the kidneys. Another bruise the size of a fist. A big, fat fist.

"I could have made him disappear, darling," she whispered in her daughter's ear, her hair brushing her face, already beginning to feel artificial, like the tails on her My Little Ponies.

He wore a flannel shirt and jeans the night Christina brought him to Park Side on Second. She had met them straight from work, her calves screaming from a day's worth of four-inch heels, her hose slicing into her abdomen. Still, this was someone her daughter loved. So she had visited the ladies' room, took the shine off her forehead and nose, refreshed her gloss, brushed her teeth from her lunch of sesame sticks.

And he couldn't bother to tuck in his shirt?

When she first spotted them at the bar, she was struck by how he stuck out among this after-hours crowd of bankers, lawyers, advertising executives. His head glowed pink beneath the pendant lamps, his thick body wedged between hands holding martini glasses and tumblers as it stretched over the bar, the cash in his paw waving in front of the bartender's nose.

Christina stood beside him, a head above the sea of gelled and angled hair. The nubby cream Chanel suit she had found in a vintage shop made her look like a newswoman, or like the public relations specialist that she was.

She closed her eyes and prayed silently. "Let him realize he's way in over his head."

When she opened them, Christina was waving frantically over the sea of gray and blue suits, tugging at the frayed sleeve beside her.

He was as unfinished a person as she had ever met, a sketch of a face that needed more detail, a lift to the chin, a narrowing of the nose. His smile too eager, his handshake too long, the grip too tight.

Christina had mentioned he did some time for threatening an ex, "but that was all behind him now, Mummy. I've helped him understand what it's like to truly be loved."

Yet Christina's eyes were telling a different story at Happy Hour that day — darting from new husband to Mummy, his paw clutching her wrist, the silent plea ambiguous.

Did she want me to love him too, or was she looking for a way out?

She knew what they must be thinking. That she had lost her mind.

Of course that's what it looks like, but here's what they don't understand: this is what she can do. It is natural to cradle your child, let her feel the comfort of shared flesh and bone, the rhythm of shared breath. Christina was still with her, she felt it. And she wasn't going to let go until she knew, without question, that what she was cradling was simply a vessel.

Christina, her beautiful ballerina, was preparing for her last dance. She was merely assisting, a familiar role.

"Oh, Jesus," one of them said.

And then a softer, gentler voice.

"It's become quite cold outside, dear, and she's wearing no clothes."

Lab Coat Woman climbed in beside her. She didn't ask her to let go of Christina, to zip the bag shut. Instead, she whispered, "They just picked him up."

She smoothed Christina's hair from her forehead, that lock so rebellious, spilling over her right eye, refusing to be tamed.

"What are we going to do about this, Mummy?" Christina, nearly as tall as she and only nine, stood in defiance at Miss Anastasia's snub. Her hands balled into fists on her slim hips, that unruly lock of hair slipping over her eye. "Surely, something can be done."

She kissed Christina's cheek with a tenderness one reserves for the very old, for the brittle. The wheels were in motion, she could assure her.

"Curtain call, darling. You're on."

Ann Elia Stewart earned a fellowship in literary fiction from the PA Council on the Arts, as well as enjoyed an extensive career in all facets of writing, including journalism, advertising copywriting, and creative nonfiction. Her work has been published by several on-line literary magazines as well as print magazines. Stewart facilitates a popular creative writing workshop for the Fredricksen Library in Camp Hill, PA and teaches creative writing at the Capital Area School for the Arts in Harrisburg, PA. Her debut novel, Twice a Child, *will be published by Sunbury Press in 2012. She lives in New Cumberland, PA, with husband Daniel, three beloved cats, Tac, Luigi and Benny, and is the proud mom of Anthony, a special makeup effects artist residing in Los Angeles.*

DRAGON RIDERS

BY
D.A. MORROW

"I don't care what you've heard, boys, there ain't no glory in riding dragons... none. Just nasty, dangerous work." The old man shakes his head slightly, scratching the long scar disfiguring the side of his face. "And never forget these brutes will try to kill you as easy as those who fly against 'em."

Tarik's voice is harsh, almost bitter, and he scowls at the children in his charge. Flickering torch light dances shadows across their faces. Not one is even sixteen, but these days, he trains what he is sent. This damn, bloody war has been going for seven years now, and the good riders—hell, even the halfway decent ones—are dead. They've been sending him little more than babies this last year. All for the King's glory.

"Nasty work... especially if you get cold easy. Saw a man lose both feet to the cold after a long fight. He torched three grays and two big blues, if you can believe it, but never flew again." His gaze burns into the small group around him. Only one, Teg, even comes up to his shoulder. Disgusting what he does for his King. But he is—has always been—a soldier, a rider for the glory of his Lord. And riders follow orders, no matter how wrong or stupid. "So keep your leathers in good repair. And keep the blankets tight."

They are standing near the broad, battered door of the keep, chill drafts seeping in and around joints and charred gaps. Last week's raid had been terrible; blood still stains the floor and walls, the stink of fire lingers in the air. They barely managed to fight off the d'Hal riders, and three good men died getting the door shut in time.

"Now, stay near me, and don't go near the damn beasts 'til I tell you." He turns, banging the ancient door with his

99

staff. The old magic works once again, and the gate slowly, grudgingly groans open.

The group walks through the shadowed entrance and onto the flattened crest of a small hill, overlooking the valley beyond. The dragon's paddock is empty, and the children cluster tight behind the old man. Icy wind gusts down from the heights, bending ever so slightly what remains of the grass. All about, jagged mountains rise steeply, their wooded sides giving way to rocky summits. Everyone agrees it is the most beautiful of the King's remaining dragon keeps, but now, all eyes drift upward.

Five boys, three girls, and an old one-legged man leaning on a staff. The best the kingdom has left. Tarik knows maybe a dozen other paddocks survived the last raids, a score at most, each with its own small flight of riders. The kingdom has what, fifty, a hundred riders left? Against how many for the d'Hal? Twice that, ten times?

Tarik shakes his head again. Isn't his concern, not now. The King's man said to get these damn children ready to fly, so that's what he will do. He'll make sure they don't die before they can be useful to their King and his cause. *Our Blessed King...*

Behind them, the door to the Rider's Keep grinds to a close, the sound echoing in the hills. All are in their flying leathers and heavy robes, and have been through their week of inside training. Learning to sit saddle on the roped barrels, to control the damned beasts in flight, to fly and not die. And the history and lore, of course, stories of brilliant battles and the great victories of the ny'Vada.

Tarik told these last tales himself, shamed, knowing the last real victory had been years ago. Now, it is a fight just to stay alive, to find enough food to eat, and forage for the dragons. The surrounding mountains have become as much their enemy as the d'Hal, and less forgiving.

But the dragons. . .that is why they are here. Today is the first time the children would meet the dragons.

A dozen blues and grays circle for a landing, released from the pens above, called down by the bells and scent of new blood and meat, scant though it is. Broad wings outstretched, the great paddle of a tail twitching the wind, they are things of grace and beauty in the air. Young, too, like the children behind him, but at least these are broken. Taught to accept the saddle and yoke, and not kill the rider. But more? Tarik hasn't had time. He never has enough time to do things right. The King was so eager to start his damnable war, so full of fancy words and promises. But time and loss, death and grief has robbed meaning from all his words.

In the beginning, Tarik was one of the King's best riders. Almost a hundred kills in the sky. He and his beautiful Bela fought from the marshes of kal'Met to the high crags of tar'Shal, until Bela was torched and he... the thoughts are too bitter to dwell on. Still, after losing his leg, he'd become the best instructor in the King's service—

A keening cry comes from above, drawing his attention back to his duty, and to the children. In front of them, landing hard, limbs splaying wide, the dragon's beauty vanishes. Tucking in their long forearms, the monsters struggle upright, deep grunts and high pitched squeals filling the paddock. Ugly, ungainly creatures on the ground, wing-fingers twisting at odd angles along their sides. They move in awkward hops to a ragged line at the near-empty blood troughs, glittering eyes betraying more hunger than interest as they inspect this new lot of riders.

Tarik moves to the head of the line, returning the creatures' gazes. Surveying the lot with a critical eye, he fears this batch is going to be even more challenging than the last.

"Dragons," he shakes his head again, talking back over his shoulder, "are the most stupid creatures the Gods ever created. I grew up on a farm, and used to think cows were bad... but they're damn geniuses compared to your average dragon."

The largest of the blues is pushing forward, away from the group, its horned head lowering, a growl coming from somewhere deep in its chest. Tarik looks at it carefully for a long moment, judging if it is the lead bull. Hard to tell, any more. Size isn't always the sign, not in the young ones. Nor is attitude—they are all vicious. During the long years of the war, the dragons have been getting younger and younger, just like their riders. And harder to train, to discipline.

The soon-to-be-riders follow a little way behind, then stop, clustering against the wind. Confidence and brave comments flowed when they were in the Keep, their pride in having been chosen as riders buoying their fear. But now, face to face with these monsters, they fall silent, and look more than a little afraid.

Each of the beasts has been fitted with a practice saddle, set low on the neck, just before the wings. High cantle and brace, the buckles lay open, ready. The lines of the yoke run through the cantle, allowing the rider to control the dragon's flight without exposing hands to the freezing winds. Seat and stirrups fit with heavy blankets, and back braces cut down to a child's size.

Tarik notices open sores along more than one wing, and shakes his head again. Whatever salves they have are for the fighting dragons. The few that remain.

A small gray on the far right lifts its tail, a low, wet, burbling noise leaking out, and everyone steps back a pace. A breeze carries the stinging odor toward the small group, and the old man makes a show of sniffing.

"And the smell! Gods! Like riding a flying fart."

They are out only a few moments when it happens.

The big blue is the lead bull after all, and as stupid as Tarik fears. Hungrier, too, for the blood troughs now hold little more than memories. Enough to ward off starvation, maybe, but just. It's swinging its head up and down the line, looking for... what? Another's share, perhaps? They are severely punished when they fight with their brethren, but that seldom stops them anymore.

The biggest boy, Teg, is showing off, moving away from the group, looking for an especially big and fearsome beast to call his own. True, it will only be a trainer, but even that is a source of pride for the new riders. Or at least for the boys... the girls are fine with the smaller beasts, and they fight as well as any. Better, many times. This war has taught Tarik much, though he doubts he will live long enough to make use of this new knowledge.

He turns his attention from the blue, inspecting the others, selecting which of his riders will get the better mounts, focusing on who showed promise in the saddle, fearing for those who will be lucky not to fall to their death the first time up.

Two dragons at the end of the line start scrapping, the bigger trying to force the smaller out of line. Tarik snaps to the trouble and starts to move, intent on interrupting before it gets out of hand. It will be very bad if they didn't get more supplies soon.

He is near the big gray when a deep-throated cough freezes his blood. What hair remains on his neck rises, and he spins, glancing back up the line, fearing he is already too late. He feels as much as sees the blue rear back, and without thinking, casts his staff at the beast. Luck or old skill brings it to the side of the blue's head, and the creature shakes itself slightly before striking.

Teg isn't stupid, and moves back when he sees the head lift, but he is too late. Gaping jaws flash down, double rows of teeth sinking into leather leggings. The boy shouts, as much in fear as pain, and the dragon rears back, shaking its muzzle roughly, like a dog with a rat. Teg flails with puny fists, doing less than no harm. The ugly maw wipes back and forth, the boy now screaming in terror.

Then, like a shot from a bow, the boy slips free from his leathers, sailing, twisting through the air, naked from the waist down, crashing hard on the sparse grass. He bounces once... twice, sliding to stillness. Frantically, Tarik hobbles to the boy's side, falling near the body, covering it as best he can with his own.

"The horns!" he screams toward the keep, "blow the damn horns!"

The blue rears again, shaking the empty leathers from its mouth, staring down at Tarik with hunger and hatred. One of the girls runs forward, hurling a stone. Another rushs headlong toward the beast, waving a cloak. For a long, agonizing moment, the big blue keeps his head high, ready to strike, selecting a morsel nearer his reach.

Then the horns sound. Great, deep, echoing blasts from the nearby walls, signaling the beasts to take to the air. The first and deepest thing taught the dragon cubs. Land

when you hear the bells, flee when the horns sound. They
are still young and stupid and hungry, but at least this
lesson has been well taught, and most back away from the
children and troughs, to the aerie's edge.

The big blue shudders, making a half-hearted lunge at
one of the girls, then lifts its head and roars. Finally, it too
breaks, dropping to the ground and slowly, grudgingly
backing away. The horns sound again, and, turning its
back, the beast flings itself from the ledge.

Gasping for air, trembling almost uncontrollably, Tarik
scans the boy beneath him. Long, angry cuts run down one
leg, bleeding freely, but shallow. The other lays twisted at a
bad angle, obviously broken. But the boy is breathing, and
his eyes flicker open. He starts to cry.

Everyone's leathers are too big, cut down from riders of
old, fitted as best they can. And that looseness has saved
his life. Maybe... At least it saved him from being eaten.

Tarik wants to scream at the boy, to beat him, to hold
him until the pain goes away. He doesn't know what he
wants. An awful, icy trembling wouldn't stop, shaking him
deep, and the cold wind cuts through him in a way it
hasn't before.

It had been too close, and it was his fault. He knows
better than turn his back on these damn brutes. He should
have kept the children with him. He knew the blue was
trouble, too, but he didn't...

Behind him, bells started ringing. And the horns. Cries
and shouts and voices growing louder as the gates slowly
swing open. A crowd gushes outward, swarming the flat
space around him and the children, ignoring them all.

"The boy," he calls to those nearest him, "help the boy."
He struggles to sit as best he can, ice-cold tremors still
racking his gut and legs. But they ignore him, dancing
instead, voices rising louder than they have in years.

He grabs the man nearest him, Ralf the saddle maker,
pulling him down. "Damn it!" he wants to hammer the
man's gapped-tooth grin, "Get help for the boy!"

But Ralf pulls away, laughing. "It doesn't matter, you
old bastard. It's over! The war is over!"

Tarik doesn't understand, can't make sense of it. The war can't be over. It will never be over. He had fought and trained and...

"Who won?" he calls to the crowd, almost desperate, trying to make his voice heard. "Who won, damn it?"

But nobody knows, no one seems to care. They only know it is over.

Moments later, two women come to his side, lifting, half carrying the boy off, shushing his tears as best they can. Overhead, dragons wheel across the sky, beautiful, graceful, confused and bewildered by the noise and activity below. They will be dangerous soon, but for now, for this briefest moment, the people near the paddock are safe.

Tarik half lays in the grass, his trembling slowly subsiding. After a time, he too starts to cry. For Teg, for his own stupidity, for his lost wife and sons, for dead friends, for his darling Bela, and soon he doesn't know why he is crying.

The tears turn to sobs, and he can't stop.

Sadly, Doug never figured out what he wanted to be when he grew up. Over the last forty years, he's been a philosopher, new-community designer, architect, project manager and educational consultant. Now, at last, as dotage draws near, he's decided to do something really challenging and become a writer.

FREE AS A BLUEJAY

BY
MADELYN KILLION

She loved to drink.

Probably a little too much, but there was no one to tell her so. And she liked that. As she sat at the bar delicately stirring her bourbon with a crooked finger, she smiled to herself. She reveled in her freedom.

Taking a sip of her drink, which she counted as the fifth of the evening, she silently pitied the others in the bar, obligated to someone or something, tethered to their families and jobs. *Not me*, she thought as she lit a Winston, *I am as free as a bluejay and just as happy.* Mitzi sucked the smoke into her fibrous lungs, holding it for a long moment. She loved smoking, perhaps even more than she loved drinking. She thought that smoking made her sexy, and she imagined men's eyes upon her as she slowly released the gray streams from her nostrils. She cast a glance around the bar, surprised that she did not catch anyone watching her. *Oh, they're good*, she thought smugly. But I can be coy, too. She raised a shaky hand to her head, unconsciously checking her hairpiece. Her hand gave it a slight pat, and then traced down her neck, feeling the wrinkles that led to the sagging flesh of her chin. *Well, what do you expect? You're sixty-six today, and bound to start aging sooner or later. Never mind the little things, she consoled herself, you still have the legs of a teenager.*

With that thought she polished off her drink and returned her attention to her cigarette. She had to buy more before the night was out. Through the haze she spied a man sitting at the opposite end of the bar. His hands clutched his half-empty glass, as if to shield it from the other patrons. He was hunched over the bar, head close to the precious glass, eyes blinking and vacant. *Poor bastard doesn't even know how pitiful he looks.*

She heaved a congested sigh, dismissing the man and his problems, and signaled to the bartender to bring her another drink. He slowly obliged, as if he were hesitant to approach her. As he did, his nose wrinkled in distaste, her cloying perfume offending him. She narrowed her eyes upon seeing this, and pursed her flaking lips. *Who the hell do you think you are? Every night I'm in this place, giving you business, and you dare to make faces?* She lifted her nose in disdain and looked away as he poured the amber fire into her glass, not giving him the chance to apologize for his rudeness. From the corner of her painted eye she saw him quickly shuffle away, distancing himself from her.

Satisfied by her silent snub, and even more satisfied by her full glass, Mitzi lit another cigarette. Her mind drifted, and she recalled past birthdays, many spent like this one, all too blurry to remember the details. *Well, old girl, at least you know how to have a good time, not like these sorry fools, too broken to lift their heads, too damn old to know when to go home. You'll never be like them, ever.*

She sipped her drink, trying to look demure, and allowed her eyes to wander the bar for another countless time. She noticed a young couple come in, stupidly giggling as they shook the snow off their coats. She watched as the man hung the damp articles on the coat rack by the door, watched as the woman watched the man. He turned with a smile to his companion, a smile that lit the room with its toothy gleam. He walked to her quickly, as if the brief moment apart from her were too much to bear, and enveloping her shoulder in the crook of his arm, guided her to a back booth.

I hope you know what you're getting into, little lady, she thought charitably. *I hope you realize they only want one thing.* She smiled a knowing smile and shook her head at the younger woman's naiveté. *You're lucky you don't have one of them to rule you, to lord over your every move. No, not you, old girl. Free as a bluejay and just as happy.* She stole a sidelong glance at the couple next to her, who had settled into their barstools soon after Mitzi's arrival. They were young as well, but that was all they shared with the two who had just arrived. These two, much to Mitzi's satisfaction, were on the brink of an argument. The young man with his hook nose and slick hair, reminded Mitzi of some of the men that she used to date in her youth, and this tangible, breathing memory sitting next to her was a reaffirmation of her sour opinion of the opposite sex. She could tell that the man was no good, and had she been the kind of person who cared about the welfare of strangers, perhaps she would have leaned over to the young woman who accompanied him and told her so. But Mitzi's shallow well of altruism was temporarily dry, so she simply sat there, a lopsided smile smeared across her face, content with the knowledge that every woman must learn these lessons for herself.

Mitzi lifted her glass to her mouth and took a long swallow. Glancing at her watch, she saw that she still had a few minutes before the liquor store closed. She could buy a bottle, buy more cigarettes. She could leave these miserable people behind. She tossed some crumpled bills on the bar and teetered to the door, pulling her threadbare coat tightly around her narrow frame. She paused before the door, and pulling out a cigarette, lit it for the walk. Heaving open the door, she stepped out of the dimly-lit bar and into the night.

She loved to drink. Probably a little too much, but there was no one to tell her so. And she liked that, she reveled in her freedom.

Eight years ago Madelyn Killion left her relatively safe job as an English teacher to enter the frontier of motherhood. Currently she lives with her two children and husband in Pennsylvania, where on any given day you can find her laughing with her family, jogging with her friends, or napping with her dog.

4:30

By
BOB WALTON

My father is a very simple man. He served in the navy during WWII. I popped into the world around the same time. The day he left for duty, he planted me in my mother's little garden. I was two-years-old when he finally made it home for good.

Dad had to clean up after battles by gathering the dead from the beaches and the water. Wherever there were dead soldiers, he'd be there afterwards. The war kept him busy. By the time his outfit reached Iwo Jima, he felt like retiring.

Dad smoked like a nervous hooker. "We all did," he would tell me. Whenever I asked why he smoked so much, "we all did" was his standard reply. He smoked for forty-seven years and finally the people who make Camel cigarettes made good on their promise.

Two days before he died my father had me sit down with him and he told me something he said he'd carried inside him for all those forty some years. He didn't breath very well at this point but he managed to get out this confession.

He called the vessel he served on a mortuary ship. It would follow the fleet around, he told me, and clean up the marines and sailors who wouldn't be making the trip home.

He said, "We had just taken the beaches of Iwo Jima; the marines were all over the place, on the beaches, inland, and on ships. And bodies were just mangled to pieces. The soldiers kept busy organizing their operations and trying to stay alive. The Japs had mines planted everywhere, including the water, and every so often you'd hear an explosion and you'd know there'd be another guy not goin' home.

"You expect people to get shot or blown up in war, and these guys had been through Hell. But I seen somethin' that day in the lagoon that made me sick to my stomach, and it's still here," he said pointing to his stomach, "in my head."

"This new troop carrier had just anchored in the bay waiting to unload its cargo of fresh marines. These guys hadn't even seen action yet." He paused. His face turned red, he looked like he was holding his breath. I asked him if he was all right. He nodded and put his fist to his chest like he had heartburn or something. I figured it had to be his heart, but said nothing. I just waited and looked at him. We both knew he wouldn't last long. Besides, what could I do for him? He looked at me hoping I wouldn't notice, like I had no idea he was sick.

"Finally," he said, "the carrier was floating near the entrance to the lagoon, when suddenly a mine hit it. When I got there, bodies were all over the place, just floating face down. There were no signs of these guys being shot, burned, or blown to smithereens. We got busy pulling them up outta the water. Some guys were down there in troop carriers scooping them up. We were droppin' nets," he stopped to catch his breath. For a couple of minutes he lay there panting. Then he continued, "...and grappling hooks, anything to get them the hell outta the water as fast as we could.

"The medics checked them. They moved from body to body quickly. One doc finally stood up and took off his helmet and scratched his head. He walked over to the Ensign in charge and said, 'But they all have broken necks.' "

Slowly my father continued, "When they were told to abandon ship, many of them were still wearing their helmets, and jumped overboard.

"Shit, son. That's at least a 40-foot drop. Do you know what their heads did when their helmets hit the water from that height?"

I didn't know if this question was hypothetical or not, but I said,

"'Uh, no."

"Their heads snapped back the second they hit the water, and broke their necks." He stopped talking and coughed, his eyes were moist from the coughing, I thought. Maybe it's the memory of those Marines "Those dumb-ass mother-fuckers never even got shot at and they died before any of 'em could shit their pants." My dad chuckled a bit. "I took off my helmet right then and there and never wore it again."

Then he coughed. He coughed good and hard. He coughed until he spat blood, and turned a couple shades of purple. Finally he settled down. My mother came in and gave him a shot of morphine the doctor had given her. We waited until he fell asleep, and left the room. That was the last thing he said. He died a couple days later in the early morning before anybody got up. My mother later told me that she thought she had heard a noise. Thinking she heard somebody downstairs she got up and went to look. She found my father at the window slouched over in the chair. His cane had knocked over the lamp.

He had been upstairs for weeks unable to even go to the bathroom. How he got downstairs beats the hell out of me. My mother still laments over that. When she saw him, she screamed bloody murder. It was 4:30 AM. I have to say he looked a lot better lying there than he had the last few weeks. It's as if all the worries left him the minute he stopped living. I don't think this could be said of the bodies he recovered in the war.

For weeks afterwards, my mother would get up at 4:30 every day like an alarm went off, go downstairs and clean the living room. But she never touched that chair again.

Robert Walton is a graduate of Penn State University, with a degree in Archeology. He has a wife, a daughter, a house, and a dog and owns his own bagel shop in suburban Harrisburg, Pennsylvania. Fatal Snow is his first completed novel and he is currently trying to sell that novel while writing a sequel called Fatal Spring (the mask of Minos).

FADE TO BLACK

BY
KATHRYN GRACE

I'm not a confrontational person. Perhaps a little hard to believe an attorney could have such a quality. But I researched my way through law school and clerkship to land my dream job writing policy and position papers about obscure points in constitutional law. No person-to-person battle ever arose. Until the day I sued my sister.

It was six years ago, but the memory of the moment that changed everything remains stark. How the sudden jangling of the phone startled me awake. My chest heavy, my heartbeat pounding in my ears, I looked at the clock: one a.m. on a Saturday.

Phone calls that wake you up are never good news. It was my brother-in-law, telling me that my nephew had been in a terrible accident and flown by helicopter to the trauma center about thirty miles from my house.

"Could you come? Janice really needs you." His voice was hoarse and broken.

"Oh my God, Don. What happened? How is he?" I scurried around my room like a frightened animal, trying to find a shirt, any shirt, hopping to pull on the the first pair of pants I touched while keeping the cell to my ear so as not to miss a word.

The voice was almost a whimper. "It's bad. He was thrown from the car. Head injury. He was having seizures at the scene. They're in with him now. We don't know anymore. Please come." He started to cry. "It was only a mile from our house. He was almost home. Please come. Oh my God, he's our only kid."

"I'm on my way," was all I could manage. I started crying; I started bargaining. "I'll believe, I'll join a church, I'll build houses for the poor, I'll never talk about anybody again, just please let him be ok."

My sister's family was my only family. Jason was an only child, the basket with all the eggs.

Somehow I got to the hospital, and to an elevator, and down a hallway and to the ICU. The floors were shiny and my shoes made clicking sounds as I followed someone in scrubs with a name tag to Room 7. The fresh smell of sanitizer and plastic, mixed with the pungent odor of vomit and urine, made my stomach turn. I stood in the doorway of Room 7, and at the far end of the room, on a bed with sheets so white his bruises stood out with even more anger, lay my nephew.

Stumbling toward him, blinking my eyes to clear the tears that gathered there to see him, the nurse pulled me back.

"He's heavily sedated. We don't want him upset. It's important for him to remain quiet."

She led me from the room to the family area, which was appropriately clean, comfortable and not too cheerful. False hopes served no purpose. Janice and Don sat there, heads down, staring at that shiny floor as if an answer to this might be written there, if only they could find it. Several other people sat there. They were all looking for that answer.

Janice looked up and then melted into my outstretched arms. I closed my eyes and felt her grief as something so physical, everything about her was heavier.

"He'll be okay," I whispered to her hair. "He's a fighter like you." For a split second, I was in a different embrace with her. The embrace after our mother died, the embrace after Janice *heard*. Then it was gone.

"There's a lot of bleeding in his brain," Doctor Trauma Surgeon said. "It will be several days until we get a better idea of the extent of his injuries, and even longer before we can comment on the permanence of any disabilities. His condition is critical. Right now we're keeping him on a ventilator and chemically paralyzed. The less stimuli he has right now, the less his brain will have to work We want the swelling in his brain to go down before we go any further. Any questions?"

"Is he going to die?"

"I can't answer that."

No more questions.

Janice and Don went in with him for a few minutes every few hours, to stand by his bed, to touch him when allowed, to watch their shared piece of life lay still and quiet except for the work of the ventilator. After five days of worsening CT scans and quiet EEG's, the traumatologist, the neurosurgeon, the pediatric neurologist all raised the possibility of stopping life support. Janice reacted as if someone had reached in with a brutal hand, right into that place in the heart where your soul lies and yanked as hard as they could. She bent slightly at the waist and circled her arms around herself as if to hold herself together. Her eyes were closed as she slowly shook her head and murmured the word 'no,' a wounded cry almost drowned out by the sound of Don falling heavily into a chair behind her.

No one challenged her. The doctors respected her decision and gave her timetables for more testing. They would talk again soon. I didn't know what to say. I looked at them both, Don with his head so low it almost touched his knees, Janice caught in her own embrace. They never touched, but waited there in those positions until the nurse came and took them back to Jason's room.

I was in awe of them both, teary-eyed in the waiting room, but up-beat at his bedside, reading to him, telling him the news, telling him jokes, trying desperately to get him to respond. I tried to be there as much as I could, taking time from my work schedule and my limited personal obligations. I tried to ease my sister's burden, although she would never let me. And so Jason stayed on life support, and they continued telling jokes. After more weeks than I can remember, they did remove the tubes. Slowly, one by careful one, because there was some brain activity. Then came the rehab hospital, where his damaged brain would try and make his body follow some basic commands. Like blink. And smile. And maybe swallow. Janice quit her job. She gave Jason everything she had, every day. But like her son, she was changed forever. And like her son, I wasn't sure what her future held.

They were together in the early stages naturally. Hospitals in particular tend to bring people closer, however artificially. As the weeks turned into months turned into a year, Jason came home. Don worked as much as possible to keep Janice and Jason there. Until the day he decided to not go back there himself. It was just too hard. Jason was so difficult to understand, and he didn't really walk without the assistance of someone and some appliances. On the rare nights when he wasn't working and he let Janice take a break, Don wheeled Jason in front of the T.V. and there he sat until Janice got back. Father and son had not been particularly close before the accident; Jason's disabilities only made it harder to connect. Janice and Don never had a very tight marital knot, and the incessant pull of lost expectations was enough to make their relationship unwind. When the marriage ended, everyone, including Janice, was disappointed.

No one, including Janice, was surprised. So Don left and moved to Canada with his travel-agent girlfriend, sending some support money and an occasional greeting card.

"It's not that much different without him," Janice would joke in the early days. "At least now I don't have to cook as much." And she kept up her spirits, and the seasons changed, and Jason got better a grain of sand at a time.

I never realized how much trouble I was in until it was too late. It was a cool April night, just after Jason's twenty-first birthday. Time and therapy had given him the ability to transfer from bed to wheelchair and from wheelchair to potty seat. With the assistance of one strong person, he could walk short distances, although it was certainly not graceful. He could feed himself slowly and sloppily if the food were cut. His speech stayed slow and monotone, very hard to understand unless you were accustomed to it. Which was a shame, because Jason was very funny. Funnier than before the accident. What he gained in humor, he lost in self-pity. His mental capacities were diminished, he would never be an engineer, but he would graduate from high school. He would make some kind of life for himself, by himself.

The problem was, he was the only one in his house who felt that way. Janice continued to care for him, never complaining and even relishing her job of keeping him safe at home. She had been against him returning to school, even though he had been determined. My job was to nudge her along the road to Jason's independence. He would call whenever she stalled, begging for help. Which was why I was in their kitchen, reading his birthday cards after he had gone to bed. Janice caught me looking at a small one that read Happy Birthday, Son.

"It had a picture of Don's two little ones in it, but I threw that away. I didn't think Jason needed to see that."

The hurt in her voice did not surprise. Neither did the alcohol on her breath. Janice had taken to having a few after Jason went to bed. I couldn't blame her. I never blamed her. Still, I should have known better than to bring up a touchy subject right then. But time was running out.

"Have you given any more thought to the group home idea?" I tried to act nonchalant.

Janice stiffened, drew herself up and back like a cobra ready to strike. "Why are you still talking about this? The answer was no, it's still no. Jason is fine right here with me. End of discussion."

"I know he's fine, but I think he would really like to try this." I took a deep breath. "And you've got to think of the long-term, Jani. What happens to him when you're not here anymore? What happens to him if something happens to you?"

I tried to keep my voice even, but it was difficult because I was afraid. I never challenged her.

Her eyes were full of venom. So was her mouth. "How dare you? How god-damn dare you? Don't you think that's all I ever think about: what's best for him? Don't you think I lie awake at night, alone, after feeding him and washing him and playing f-ing checkers with him and worry myself to sleep thinking about what's going to happen to him when I'm gone? I'm all he has, I'm all there is to depend on. You think you can waltz in here to put in a little time and think you're helping me. You think you can just take him out and drop him off somewhere where nobody knows him and he'll be just fine? He won't be fine. He'll never be fine. He needs to be with me. I'm his mother. Not you."

She was breathing hard and turning red. She took a long gulp out of a tall glass. Her words stung, as she meant them to. I wasn't anyone's mother, probably never would be. But I couldn't let go, not this time. My head buzzed. The clock ticked louder than it should have. The birthday card blew off the table with a gust of April air.

"Who are you doing this for Jani?" I stopped for just a second, fearful, because I was about to say things that might make her never speak to me again. "You're being selfish. You need him more than he needs you right now. What are you afraid of? That he's going to leave you too? That someone can get along without you? He's your son Janice. You've done everything for him. He'll always love you. Just like —"

"Just like mom? Forget it. He's staying with me." She was quiet now, almost whispering.

"I was going to say, he'll always love you, just like me."

The quiet was shattered, like her glass as she threw it against the wall. "Get out."

In a minute we heard the sound of the wheelchair motor. "What's all the noise? Can't an invalid get a good night's sleep around here?" He entered the room, looking nervously at our faces.

"Sorry we woke you. You know how your aunt gets when we talk politics. She was just leaving when I dropped my glass. You can go back to bed." We both knew he heard, but we all pretended he had not.

"It's about the group home, isn't it?" Jason looked uncomfortable, but put himself between Janice and I. "I'd really like to go see it, Mom. Won't you take me?"

"That's where people go who have no one else to take care of them honey. And you have me." She bent forward to kiss his head.

"But I'd really like to at least see it. I'm twenty-one now. Don't you want to get rid of me and find a boyfriend?" He smiled wickedly his somewhat lopsided smile.

Janice didn't bite. "No, I don't want to get rid of you, and the last thing I need is a boyfriend. I'm having a hard enough time dealing with my family right now, let alone a boyfriend." That comment was not lost on Jason or I. I moved toward the door.

"Don't be mad at her, Mom. I started it. I really, really want to go. " Jason moved his wheelchair to block the door. "The counselor at school talked to me. He thought it was a great idea too. He said he would talk to you. Mom, I'm graduating next month. I want to start planning what to do with life. You need to have a life too. I want to be something other than a guy in a wheelchair."

Because you had to concentrate so hard on what he was saying, and it took so long for him to speak, the mood had changed by the time Jason was done.

"If you don't get to bed, maybe you won't graduate." Janice said this lightly as she went for the broom. "Be careful over here, there's glass on the floor."

"Everyone bosses the disabled guy," I heard him mumble as he headed out of the kitchen.

"Janice?"

"Don't. Push. Me. Get out or I swear I will call the police. Get out before I hurt you."

She spoke very calmly, and surprised as I was, I left immediately.

Graduation day arrived, and clutching my invitation written in Jason's shaky hand, I stood in the back of the auditorium alone and misty-eyed, as Jason received his diploma to a standing ovation from a class of seniors who were in fifth grade when he first started high school. I spotted Janice near the front, looking proud, as well she should. Jason gave a short speech, thanking everyone for helping him and believing in him, especially "the girls who did my math homework for the last three years." He gratefully thanked his Mother, the person who really saved his life, the one he could never have done any of this without, and the one who was going to help him start a new part of life today, another commencement. Everyone clapped and cried, including me, although I didn't think they could understand most of it.

I remember the terrible feeling of isolation I carried, removed from my sister, divorced from the only family I had, guilt already moving slow and warm inside of me like a first sip of brandy.

Jason was going to start a new life, whether Janice wanted it or not. I had not spoken to her since the night in the kitchen, but I had spoken to Jason. When he turned eighteen, Janice had proudly let him remain competent in the eyes of the law. Competent to make his own decisions, even though he couldn't carry them out on his own. Competent, with the aide of a good lawyer, to move out from under the sheltered blanket of his mother before he smothered.

And I was a good lawyer.

I left the graduation without seeing Janice or Jason. He would tell his mother the following day of his plan to move out. If she resisted, he would call the school counselor who would come and talk to her. If she still refused, he would call me and I would try and explain the legal situation to her. If she still refused, I would start the process anyway. She would fight, but it would be to no purpose. Any attorney would tell her that, including me.

None of this was done in anger, I told myself. None of it with bitterness for the life Jason might lose, or the life I had lost. When our mother lay dying, our father had left long before, she told me I was special. That I would be someone who would make a difference, save the world maybe. That she loved me more than anyone, even more than my sister, who drove our father away. And as she told me this and closed her eyes for the last time, I saw the movement from the corner of my eye. Janice was there. She had heard. I stood up and hugged her tightly. Her weight was crushing. We never spoke of it: the hurt, the betrayal. But I lived it. I spent my life trying not to be special, making Janice special, loved, in control, because of the guilt I felt over being loved more. Because of the fear I had that the one person left in this world with me would think I believed what our mother had said. I would show her by the way I lived my life that I didn't think I was any of those things.

I let Janice pick my career, my law school even. She found me my job, close by her and Don so that we could always spend time together. She talked me out of boyfriends and a bad engagement. And I let her. Until now. Now I stood ready to change all that, and except for my fear and my guilt and my sadness, I would.

The phone rang. "If you do this, we are done. If you do this, I will kill you." It was Janice, badly slurring her words. She had lost it when Jason told her, so much so that he had packed a few things with my help when Janice was out and was now staying at the group home, awaiting the judge's order. He loved it, but was in anguish over his mother.

"She's angry and drinking every time I talk to her." He told me this the day before. "Please help her."

"She'll be okay, Jay." I didn't really believe this. "She's just scared for you and for herself. But this is all about you. It's your life. She'll come around."

"You make it sound okay. You make it sound normal. All kids my age move away from home. And all the moms hate it." The excitement returned to his voice. "But you're right. They all get over it. Let's do this. I rock."

I clenched the phone hard as I mentally returned to Janice. "Do you want to talk about this? I'd really like to talk."

"There's nothing to talk about. He's my son. Mine. He needs me and loves me. And I love him. More than anything in the world." Whether she said this on purpose or not, the words sounded hauntingly familiar. I waited for the click. It didn't come.

She was waiting for me to crumble, again.

"Jani, Janice. There are a few things you need to understand." I used my quiet, lawyer voice, the one I used in the library. "I am not doing this. He wants this. He needs this. And he's going to get it. If you come to court tomorrow, you are going to lose. Second, you are right, he loves you more than anyone in the world." My voice caught. "Just like I do. Third. Don't ever threaten me again. See you in court." It was the first time I had ever hung up on her. I felt exhilarated. I felt ashamed. I picked up the phone and put it down again. I felt special.

I slept better than I had in months, confident in what the next day would bring. Something good, I was sure of that. I would make sure. Janice would be crushed, but in time she would see that it was for the best. She could decide to hate me forever, but I didn't think she would. We were family, after all, and had been through things together that many wouldn't see in a lifetime. I was helping Jason start a new, exciting life. When I left the house, I had purpose. And a new suit, a briefcase and a determination to show everyone there the amazing lawyer I always was.

Only I never got to show anyone. Court was scheduled for 9 am. I arrived early, to shuffle through my papers, greet all the character witnesses as they came in. Jason took the van from the group home, partly to show the judge, and partly to show his mother, that he could get around on his own. A few news people hung around; the case had made the papers, but luckily it wasn't front-page news. It was getting warmer. I took off my jacket, still smelling new. The judge asked for a second cup of coffee. A reporter left.

At nine twenty-five, still no Janice. The judge was talking contempt. Her attorney continued to make phone calls while Jason became increasingly worried. I snuffed the impulse to feel smug. She knew she had lost. It was the first time I wouldn't let her win, and she couldn't stand it. But I would forgive her, for everything. We would all move on, having grown and matured through this painful experience.

At nine thirty-two, the court deputy escorted in a state trooper who said Janice had lost control of her car and run head-on into a utility pole. Dead at the scene. Alcohol was present on the scene. As was an unregistered, but loaded, hand-gun.

Kathryn Grace is a Central Pennsylvania native. Although she works in orthopedic surgery, she dreams of being a writer.

THE NATURE OF SIN

By
MARIA McKEE

"Memorize these stages of sin," Sister Avila admonishes my sixth-grade Sunday school class.

The room is warm and the class is restless. Sister claps her hands. "Pay attention!

"First, you are tempted. Second, you keep thinking about what tempts you, and lastly, you commit the sin. What is sin? Sin is a mockery of God."

Sister takes several deep breaths. The large starched white bib on her chest rises and falls; her cheeks redden. She's warmed to the subject, anticipating her next words.

"Heed this, children!" she shouts. "God will *not* be mocked! Ask the Almighty to make you impervious to temptation. Remember our God sees everything you do."

Thwack! We all jump as she whacks her desk with a ruler.

"What you do has *consequences!* Most sinners forget this."

Sister reaches for her rosary and brandishes the crucifix around the room like a spiritual divining rod, poised to quiver at the tempted or the already-fallen. When she stops, the crucifix is pointed at me.

Sister's lesson has come too late: I had already sinned. Most definitely.

At the moment, I felt rather good about it.

Sunday mornings my sister Teddy and I walked downtown to Catechism and Mass. We passed department store displays filled with all manner of things for sale: toys, radios, televisions, band instruments, mannequins wearing the latest fashions and jewelry, treasures enough to lure a pirate from his ship. I couldn't resist window-shopping.

I was content enough to daydream until the Sunday I paused before a display of girl's shoes with pencil thin one-and-one-half inch high heels. The universe tilted. I felt stunned. Lightheaded. Speechless. In love. A large sign called them kitten heels. "These tiny trainer heels are the first step in your daughter's becoming a young woman." *I had to have a pair.*

Then cold sanity washed over me, and my universe righted itself. How would I acquire the shoes, given that all the desires in my life had to first pass through the omnipotent evaluation and quality control system called Mother? I planned my strategy during Mass.

I didn't know how the girls who wore kitten heels had convinced their mothers, but in dealing with mine, I'd learned to anticipate her objections and have answers ready.

She'd surely cite safety and cost. If I could convince these were needless worries, I stood a good chance of success.

Talking points fixed in my mind, I approached her.

"No," she said, "not a good idea."

"Why?" I asked, knowing full well her objection.

"Because you'll twist your ankle or fall."

This was going just as I'd expected. I continued in a calm, confident manner.

"But, compared to the stilettos—you know those really, really—*really*—high heels, the kitten heels I want are low to the ground." I showed her the measurement on a ruler.

Mistaking her silence for acquiescence, I forged on. "All the girls are wearing them, and they aren't twisting their ankles, which means *other* mothers think the heels are safe. And besides that, you won't have to buy me school shoes. I can use my Sunday shoes for everyday."

Mama shook her head, not impressed by my impassioned plea, nor one to be swayed by other-mother peer pressure.

"No."

"But why can't I have the heels? Give me a reason... please?" A whine crept into my voice. "I'm the *only* one that still has to wear baby shoes." My confidence and bravado vanished. I'd promise anything if she granted me this desire. "I'll...I'll—"

Mama interrupted. "The reason is because I said so, and being the only one isn't a bad thing—it shows how sensible you are."

Sensible? I wanted to be glamorous and grown-up. Sensible had no room in my pre-teen vocabulary. "But—"

She held up her hand. "End of discussion."

Disappointed and desperate, I appealed to my father.

"You want a kitten?" he asked, laying his newspaper aside. "I don't think your mother would like that. Cats can be destructive."

"No, Daddy, I'm talking about shoes with *kitten* heels."

"Shoes with kittens for heels? *What* are you talking about? Is this some kind of horrible new fad?"

I sighed and described the shoes again.

He glanced at my feet. "What's wrong with the shoes you have?"

Before I could explain, he shook his head. "Kitten shoes...what's next? Dogs? Go ask your mother. She knows about these things." He picked up his newspaper and disappeared behind it.

With my last hope dashed, I should have given up, yet I couldn't stop thinking about the shoes, and the more I thought, the greater grew my longing. Throughout the summer I left nose prints on shop windows all over town, but in terms of fueling the flames of desire, most of my coveting took place after I'd received communion. While I kneeled in prayer posture with my head bowed piously, anyone who might randomly have looked at me, would have seen that my eyes were not focused on matters spiritual, but were instead riveted on the passing parade of feet. I scrutinized the shoes for my favorite colors and the most popular styles, and with each gaze, I became more entrenched in the first and second stages of sin.

One Sunday during shoe review, my heart sank even more. I had overlooked a crucial need: hose. I couldn't wear heels with the lacy white ankle socks my mother favored. I prayed, and God responded with not one, but two miracles.

My aunt gave me a pair of hose for my birthday. Though I had zero expectations Mama would allow me to wear the nylons, she gave her permission, begrudging though it was.

"Busybody—that's what your aunt is. I told her I didn't want you to wear nylons, and she had the nerve to argue with me. Thinks she knows everything because she raised six girls. Your *dear* father took her side.

"Go on then, wear the nylons, but if you tear them, I'm not buying you another pair. Guess I'll have to make you garters."

Pleased as I was with the hose, I bemoaned how, paired with my dumpy lace-up oxfords, the effect was less than elegant.

"Mama, these nylons look stupid with my shoes. Please, won't you change your mind about the heels? Please?"

Elegance was not on Mama's priority list. The hose and garters had been her last concession. "No heels."

I prayed and waited for another heavenly intercession. Nothing happened. I supposed God doled out a finite number of miracles, and I had met my quota. If I wanted the shoes, I was on my own. I hatched a scheme to get them, and thus, passed the point where it would still have been possible to avoid the slippery slope into sin.

My plan was simple, but a major obstacle stood in the way: money. My sister was the answer. I nonchalantly proposed my idea to her on our walk to church.

"I want to buy a pair of shoes. I have eight dollars. If you lend me two dollars and fifty cents, I'll have enough to buy the shoes. I'll pay you back"

"Are these the shoes you and Mama have been arguing about?"

"Yes. So?"

"You can't buy those shoes—she won't let you wear them."

"Thought of that."

Our Catechism class met in the elementary school across the street from the church. Since Teddy and I walked to Sunday services, we always allowed extra time so we didn't need to hurry. That extra time would by my ally.

"I'll hide the shoes in the garage where Mama won't find them, and I'll take them with me on Sundays. When we get to the school, I'll go to the girls' room and change into my new shoes. After Mass, I'll go back to the bathroom and put on my old shoes. Not a bad plan, if I say so myself."

"Well? What about the money?"

"I don't know...you'll get caught," Teddy warned.

"No I won't. Not if you don't tell."

"I won't tell, but think about other times. You always get caught."

"Yeah, but those were other times," I countered. "Just don't tell."

"I won't, but sooner or later..."

"Decision time. Are you going to lend me the money, or not?"

"I might...it *depends*." Teddy arched her eyebrows.

"*Oohh!* What do you want?" I asked, amazed at how fast she'd found a way to blackmail me.

"I want to ride your bike—whenever I want it—for the rest of the summer, and let's see...I also want to read the new *Nancy Drew* before you do." Teddy flashed a smug gotcha-grin. "Promise, or no deal."

"Deal. But remember, if you snitch, I'll tell Mama you broke her necklace."

Cavalier in her advantage, Teddy shrugged. "I won't tell, but you'll get caught."

Later that week, under the guise of going to the playground, I snuck downtown and bought the shoes.

My plan went without a hitch for nearly two months. I wore the shoes, puffed with pride, finally an equal with the other girls.

But the God who dispenses miracles, is also the God who will, after all, not be mocked.

After Mass I dash out of church, intent on crossing the street to the school.

Light rain falls, spattering my shoes. *Oh, no!* I think. *They'll get water spots.* I run.

The drizzle acts like wax on the worn church steps. I slide. My right heel catches the edge of a step. *Yikes!* Unbalanced! I can't control my feet! I flail my arms.

Suddenly my hand brushes against something, and I grab it like a drowning person catching a thrown lifeline. But this lifeline doesn't save me. I fall.

Thud! Ouch! Crack! Crunch! *Rippppp!* A piercing scream. People shouting. People running.

When I catch my breath, I open my eyes. Prone on the cement, I'm relieved I'm not mortally wounded and that all my limbs feel intact. I have an intimate view of people's legs. Wadded in my white-knuckled fist is a flowered pale blue and white cloth.

The trail of fabric leads to a woman sitting splayed-legged on a church step, the lower half of her dress torn from the bodice; the material is stretched between her legs and my hand, taut as a tightrope. Her pillbox hat rests on the rim of her glasses. She pushes it back, looks around, and is greeted by the susurrus of surprised mutterings from the crowd gawking at her exposed legs, garter belt and underwear.

"Oh, my God!" she utters as she tries to cover herself with one hand while tugging at the fabric I still clutch with her other hand.

I rest my head on a step and envision God shaking His finger at me, shouting,

"I will not be mocked!" He sounds like Sister Avila. Perhaps it *was* Sister.

She hurries down the steps, and blesses herself. After she pries the dress from my hands, she shouts for someone to help me up.

Teddy arrives. "Oh boy! Are you ever going to get it!"

She picks up my missal, then points. "Look!"

The right heel, rent from my shoe, has landed at the base of the step, eerily upright and apropos of nothing. My heart sinks. My beautiful shoes, ruined. Tears trickle down my face.

Sister Avila peers over her spectacles. "Stop crying. You're fine. We'll drive you and your sister home, and you can tell your parents what happened." She motions for the woman and her husband to follow her.

The grim delegation that greets my mother causes *her* universe to wobble. Shocked first by the disheveled woman wearing a torn dress, fastened with a dozen safety pins from the waist to bodice, she shrieks upon seeing me dirty and barefoot. "Holy Mother of God! What's happened?"

127

She takes a step toward me, but I step back and hide myself behind Sister Avila's ample form.

Mama hollers for my father. "Ray!"

Sister moves aside, and my mother yanks me forward. Her hands hold my shoulders in a death grip.

"Rayy-mond!"

My father comes running, sees everyone and asks, "What is it? Has there been an accident?"

"Nothing serious, praise the Lord," says Sister Avila. "Carmen fell on the church steps and broke a heel on her shoe."

Sister points to the shoes I hold. "She can tell you the rest."

My parents lean closer, look at the shoes, then at me.

"*Where* did you get those shoes?" Daddy asks.

Enumerating my transgressions to an audience in broad daylight makes kneeling before a priest in a darkened confessional seem like a cake walk. I wish I could turn back the clock; I want to run away, but I can't do either. I tell the entire story, omitting nothing, while Sister mumbles under her breath and fingers her rosary beads.

She taps my head with her divining rod crucifix. "Disobeying your parents, sneaking around. Lying. What you did is a sin. Go to confession."

My father pays the woman for her torn dress and hose, and they leave.

I stand shame-faced before my parents. As Sister had avowed in her Sunday school lesson, most sinners forget about consequences, and indeed, until now, I'd given consequences little regard. I desire the refuge of the confessional and the priest's predictable penance. My parents' punishment will neither be predictable nor easy.

"Go to your room and write apology notes—including one to your mother and me," Daddy orders. "Stay there until we decide what to do with you."

My parents' favorite punishment was house arrest. During the thirty-one days of my confinement, I was forbidden to talk to my friends on the phone, watch TV, or listen to the radio. All the dishes, ironing and scrubbing the floors were mine to do without help. Sister Avila also benefited. Once a week, for the following year, I had to help her assemble care packages for the needy.

My sister got off easy despite aiding and abetting me. My parents concluded that, although she had acted wrongly, she was younger, meaning I had coerced her. Although I didn't have to repay her, I still had to compensate my parents.

In the immediate hubbub of that Sunday's events, I'd forgotten to return to the girls' room for my oxfords; when I went to retrieve them, they were gone. I had to wear sneakers to church. Another year passed before I could afford to purchase new hose.

Teddy showed no mercy. She called in her chit, seizing my bicycle whenever she wanted it, and claiming first reading rights to the latest *Nancy Drew* mystery. Unable to resist gloating, she often reminded me of her warnings. "Told you so. Told you so. Told you so!"

"Shut up."

To Dad's credit, he tried several times to glue the severed heel, but it resisted adhesion, and he gave up. Mama tossed the shoes into the garbage.

Shoe losses, the woman's dress and hose reimbursement, plus what I owed my parents for Teddy's loan, put me forty dollars in debt. In those days, when a loaf of bread cost a mere fifteen cents, forty dollars seemed like untold wealth. My piggy bank remained empty for the year it took me to repay every cent.

Fifty years have passed, but even the haze of time hasn't erased the image of Mama throwing my beloved kitten heels into the trash.

She'd shaken her finger at me. "Let this be a lesson."

I *had* learned a lesson, but not the one either my mother or Sister Avila would have anticipated.

I confessed as ordered, and as I recited the list of my offenses, tried to evoke sincere contrition. Yet, in the deepest recesses of my heart, lurked the truth: I wasn't genuinely remorseful, only sorry I'd gotten caught.

I *had* sinned. Most definitely. While I'd worn those lovely slip-on Pandora's boxes, I hadn't cared. I felt *wonderful!*

"And that, Sister Avila," I would tell her if I could, "is the *nature* of sin."

Maria McKee is a reclusive Virgo. Occasionally she ventures out to the grocery store or to a shoe store. If you happen to see Maria, speak to her at your own peril. Everything you say or do is fodder for her fiction.

DEAD LETTERS

BY
SUSAN GIROLAMI KRAMER

Mary refused to throw away the yellowed newspapers, chipped coffee cups, vintage fabric, disheveled books, and piles of photographs of unknown people in every corner of her apartment. *She'll be furious when she realizes what I have done.*

I bit my nails as I waited for her over an hour at the back door to my Laundromat, anxious about the confrontation about to happen. My parents took Mary in when, as an infant, she was left at their doorstep. They never really labeled her mental disability, only saying Mary needed our family to be hers. It took time, but I got used to her eccentricities.

I only moved back into the area to help her and give her a job at the Laundromat. She refused at first, saying she couldn't leave the post office, but Mary became so good at filling the laundry orders for local hotels, my business started to boom.

I went outside to smoke, finishing about three cigarettes when I heard my name being called.

"I wondered where you were." The young college student smiled at me. I had hired her to make lattes and cappuccinos at the Café I opened next door to the Laundromat.

"The sign is up and looks fab," she said.

"So it's official now, I have my own business:'Love's Cafe & Laundromat.'"

"Unusual Mary's not back from her weekend with Betty. Have you seen her?"

"No, I haven't."

I snuffed my last cigarette butt into the ground and tensed at feeling a hard stare. I looked up at the back window of Mary's apartment above the Laundromat. She opened the window and threw out the old books I had given her last Christmas.

The books landed right at my feet.

"Mary, we need to talk, meet me in my office, now," I yelled.

I picked up the books, their spines now completely broken. I went to my office and heard squeaking coming towards me.

Mary wheeled a rusty, upright cart in front of me. The cart overflowed with shoeboxes of junk. I sighed.

"Try and understand why I had your clutter cleaned out, only the stuff that could be a hazard," I said like a parent scolding her daughter for not taking better care of her belongings.

"I'm hurt you'd do that without asking," Mary sniffled, tears forming.

"Glad I took the most important things with me over the weekend. You won't get my cart and my letters," she said with confidence.

"Letters? What letters?" I frowned. Mary opened a box marked Dead Letters scrawled on the front and held them at arms length.

"Let me hold them."

"No, no one holds them but me. I'm not sharing with you," she said.

I peeked into the box and glanced at the thick lines blotting out the name of the person to whom the letters were addressed. No return address and hardly enough information for whom the letter was intended.

"Where'd you get these?"

"Betty found them, ready for the shredder, and read them, said they belonged to me." Mary placed the box carefully on top of some frayed burlap fabric.

"She took these before her last day at the post office?"

"Supposed to shred them, but couldn't when she read them. She always read them before disposing. I read them, and they're mine now." Mary started to leave.

"Mary you have to get rid of the cart, it's too obnoxious and gaudy," I called to her.

She stopped only to grumble, "No way, helps me watch over my treasures."

Every time I stared at her cart too long, she'd frown and move it far away from me. I watched her show a select few the worn handwriting, and to others, reveal bits and pieces of their lost words.

After a few days, I couldn't wait any longer. So I eavesdropped while Mary confided in the young barista at the cafe, that she thought the letter writer could be her mother.

"I often picture our life together if you had chosen me. Sometimes I wish I knew exactly where you were, so I could claim you for my own. I wouldn't be afraid.

Do you remember telling me that you never felt so in love? I know in my heart you think about me every day as I do you. You deserve a woman who can only love you like I do and bear you children. I hope these letters find you. I will keep writing until they do. Forever, A."

Mary held the letter to her chest. "This has to be my mother, she tried to find my father to make us a family. He must have known Richie and Barbra Love to leave me with them."

I slid behind the counter and brought the pot out to offer Mary a refill. She jerked at seeing me and knocked over her cup, sending splatters of coffee on her letter.

"Dottie, look what you've done," Mary said getting up and wiping the stains off her letter with her sleeve.

"Mary, I'm sorry, please allow me to read the letters or read them to me." My eyes pleaded.

"Maybe," is all she said and wheeled out of the cafe building.

I bowed my head in defeat for now.

The sounds of the Laundromat—machines buzzing, dinging, and clinking— followed me around as I walked through it to go outside and view the signs.

Mary followed me out with her cart. "Beautiful, aren't they?" I said.

"Colorful," she said wheeling her cart back and forth like she needed to calm a crying baby in its carriage.

Mary wore her usual denim skirt, braided hair, and red polo. Her new glasses magnified her eyes like a microscope making the minute viewable.

The vanilla latte I had in place of breakfast gurgled going down my empty stomach. "How's the letter reading going?"

"It's coming along. I won't hold a grudge too much longer," Mary smiled.

"Good, I want to know what you find out about your birth parents. I've always wondered where you came from."

"Maybe you can help?" Mary said and headed toward the former Laundry Mill building, now the cafe, with several old washers and dryers in the back for the laundry we did for hotels in the area.

Just as the door opened to go back in the Laundromat, I heard some commotion.

A few customers looked frazzled. Sparks started to fly like fireworks. A dryer made a rumbling sound like a car before it dies, and left off steam from its door. I helped a young woman untangle her myriad of thongs, lace bras, and silky pillowcases, out and into another dryer.

That dryer started to shake and putter. I smelled something burning. Then a man pointed at one of the massive front-loader washers, heaving, then shaking so hard, its glass door popped open.

Someone screamed watching flames consume her jeans and T-shirts. I called the fire department immediately as people started to run from the building.

Mary and the barista rushed in to help get people out. Smoke started to puff out of the dryers, setting the smoke alarms screeching over the sound of the fire truck sirens.

I stood outside with a handful of people curious how new machines could break down so quickly. A fireman approached and asked to speak with me privately. He estimated the cause was faulty wiring in the whole building and that all machines would need replaced. My heart sank. I had flyers made for my official grand opening next week.

It could take a month or more until we're up and running again. Mary placed her hand on my shoulder after I told her the news.

"You'll have to stay with me for a while," I said. Mary squinted her eyes and pursed her lips. I remembered that look growing up, when my parents didn't give her the answer she wanted.

"I'll finish doing the hotel laundry, here's my key, take the rest of the day off," I said.

I watched Mary cross the street to walk the few blocks to my house, not realizing at first that she didn't have her cart.

When I went to the back of the cafe that housed the leftover washers and dryers, I spotted her cart with white lights intertwined within the metal grates and illuminating it as though it were a Christmas decoration.

I wasted no time and opened up the box of letters. Finally, I could hear the lost words of a stranger. I shuffled them around like playing cards and closed my eyes as I chose one to read first.

As I read, I loaded a washer of white hotel towels. "Phew, Clorox, too much of a good thing," I said out loud.

The humming sound of the washer provided background music as I opened more of the letters. I became entranced, losing track of time.

Suddenly, Mary stood in the doorway. I became startled, and opened the washer door and threw in the box of letters.

Letters soon were smacking up against the glass door of the washer, words bleeding away. I held my hands to my mouth.

Mary opened up the hatch and dug her hands in the machine. "The letters, what did you do Dottie?" she screamed.

She scooped out what looked like oatmeal. I trembled. "I'm so sorry, I panicked."

Mary didn't answer, she continued to bail out the rest of the soggy letters, sobbing uncontrollably.

"I'll make it up to you somehow." I tried to console her. She pushed me away.

"This is all I had left of my parents."

Fumes from the Clorox wafted by me, lingering around my face. "No, it can't be, I'll help you find out who your parents were."

135

Mary stomped her feet on a pile she made of letter scraps on the floor. "Did you read them all?"

"No, didn't finish."

"Then you don't know," she kicked around the pile.

"What don't I know?" I said, thinking she was playing with me.

"Your Aunt."

"My Aunt Toni? Are you saying she's your mother? No way." I picked up a broom to sweep away the mess.

"She's your mother too."

"Stop your lying, you know that's not true."

"I've made copies of all the letters. I found out that Daddy Love is our father, he and his wife couldn't have children and he wanted to have children," she said so matter-of-fact.

The words circled to the front of my mind, like an advertisement trailing from an airplane in the sky. Tears flowed down my puffy cheeks. *Mary my sister? My father unfaithful to my mother? They were never apart.*

I looked up at Mary unable to speak, and for the first time, noticed her wide smile resembled my father's.

Susan Girolami Kramer wears many hats at her job as a communications specialist and at home. She's a photographer, fiction writer, editor, graphic designer, published news and fiction writer; and serves as Rose and Thorn's Journal Newsletter *producer, an online literary journal. Susan is currently working on a novel.*

DISSIPATION

BY
C.A. MASTERSON

The air is tinged with effervescence, it occurs to me as I hold the car door open. Ann slinks inside, graceful and treacherous and perfect, like a jaguar warily settling on a limb. The neon orange-purple sky glows for a few moments like a stratospheric light show. Like a good omen.

I don't even mind the crush of strangers as we wait outside the theater. I've looked forward to this concert for weeks – it marks a move forward, out of the haze of gloom I've been mired in for too long. Ann leans into me; I swear I can feel her bare skin through my shirt. She doesn't notice; her long fingers adjust a strand of hair just so behind her ear. I want to lean into her and nip her ear lobe, but settle for running my hand down the small of her back. She smiles, but her eyes have that predatory look, as if I were a moth alighting on her newly spun web that glistens in the moonlight. But oh how it glistens! And I want to be caught.

People are glommed onto the theater, onto each other. We're in the center of a crush of bodies, being sucked inside, then dispersed within.

Ann asks if I've been here before.

Just once, I tell her, but don't say with who. I don't want to mention her name, spew it into the atmosphere, where it might reverberate in the night as it's been reverberating through my head for weeks. Saying Yasmine's name will conjure images: her smile, the smell of her hair, the texture of her skin.

I smile at Ann. She's the extreme opposite of Yasmine, alphabetically and otherwise. Ann, I think, I can handle. The couple of dates we've been on, I think I've zeroed in on her inner workings. It wasn't difficult. She likes all things trendy – this might be either challenging or ultimately boring; I normally don't follow trends, not like I suspect

Ann does. She only likes popular music, she sings along without comprehending the words. Even when sung in a gut-wrenching scream, the lyrics slide right off her, like her slinky clothes. But once you've gotten that far, nothing else matters.

We sit down, and when the lights dim, I feel a rush. I check Ann for any similar signs of anticipation, but she's watching some latecomers take their seats.

I almost didn't invite her tonight. I'd bought these tickets months ago, when I was still with Yasmine. She'd gotten so excited that these three musicians were coming to town that I bought the tickets online that day. They're amazing, she'd said. Unique.

That's exactly how I think of Yasmine – amazing, unique. But also challenging, on lots of levels. It was such a struggle sometimes just to have a conversation without it turning into something socio-political. My consciousness had to be at its uppermost heights at all times in order to even be in the same vicinity as Yasmine's. It felt too much like work, sometimes, to maintain that level of purity in thought and spirit. I'm just not that pure.

When the stage lights come up, the classical guitarist, pianist and bassist step into the spotlights and introduce themselves to applause. The pianist nods at the others, and they begin an intricate melody that nearly lifts me out of my seat. The bassist's hands caress the curves of the oversized instrument as if it were a woman, and the way he moves with the bass, it nearly looks alive. The guitarist's fingers skitter up and down the frets, both hands moving like spiders on the neck of the acoustic guitar. The pianist's hands are a blur as he sways back and forth with the rhythm. When the melody ends, I clap, begging for more.

Why aren't they singing? Ann asks.

It's all instrumental. I told you that.

I thought that was their name. Her mouth is pouty.

Just listen, I tell her. *Let the music carry you away.*

I wish, she says, but her hands clench the ends of the armrests, like she's in for a rough ride.

I ignore her theatrics. My eyes search the faces of those scattered around me in the dark theater. Couples nod at each other enthusiastically, some just watch the musicians eagerly.

Then I see Yasmine. Her seat is three rows in front of ours, to the right of the stage. I force myself to turn back to the musicians as they begin the next song. I don't want to look at her. I don't know why she's here. She shouldn't be here.

It was my final revenge, keeping these tickets after we split up. She'd wanted to see this group, not me, though I later listened to their CD and couldn't stop. I'd play it in the car, at home, wherever I could. It was the only way I could lose the terrible feelings that were churning inside me. The music was soothing to my soul, it filled the echoing chasm Yasmine had left. Some nights the chasm transformed to an abyss that nearly swallowed me. But the music always levitated me, always saved me.

Now it's all crashing down again. I can't keep my eyes off Yasmine. She's listening so intently as the guitarist pinches and squeezes the notes, she winces at the sad strains, then her mouth opens in a surprised smile as the music flies into a wildly ecstatic melody.

How much longer? Ann asks.

Should be an intermission soon, I tell her, my smile sour.

I lean forward. My jaw tenses. Yasmine is mesmerized, so caught up in the music she'll never look in my direction. Her eyes follow the music to whichever player is spotlighted.

Then everyone's clapping, and the house lights come up.

Oh good, Ann says. *I need a drink.*

I shuffle behind her, stealing glances across to the next aisle as Yasmine smiles at the guy she's with, talking excitedly. She's elated to be here. Of course she'd be here, I tell myself. I should have expected it. My ego told me she'd never come, she'd avoid the concert to avoid me.

Ann heads straight for the bar, and gives me an expectant look. I follow to pay for her drink.

Let's go outside, she says, seeing others outside smoking.

I want to grab a CD, I tell her.

Okay, come out when you're done. She doesn't wait for an answer. She's already walking toward the door, flipping on her cell phone. It rings immediately, and it's like an alarm bringing her out of her cryogenic boredom to animation once again – her arm flails as she speaks, pacing, nodding; stopping to sip her drink, she taps her foot.

Watching her, I feel my neck grow thick like a tree trunk, my legs stiffen, and my shoes take root on the carpet. Everything feels so wrong, out of control, people are whirling around me like I'm surrounded by a cyclone.

In the reflection of the glass-front building, I see Yasmine walking toward me. My neck extends like a turtle from its hard shell, my roots snap as my body turns toward her. But she's looking at her companion, and shines her warm smile on him instead of me.

I walk dejectedly to the end of the line to buy a CD, keeping my eyes on the floor, on the person in front of me, anywhere but on Yasmine, so I won't have to see her with someone else.

I try to remember the exact turn of events leading to our breakup. It began with something small and stupid, exacerbated by stubbornness. She wanted to go to some artsy foreign film, I wanted to go out dancing. It escalated, spiraled uncontrollably out beyond our reach until we both said things that were meant to cut to the bone, to weaken the spirit of the other. We'd been talking about moving in together. Maybe I wasn't ready, then, and wanted to buy some time. I didn't know what I had. Seeing her tonight, comparing her to Ann – it's like comparing an orchestral warmup to a symphony. One's just going nowhere.

I pay for the CD – it's their new one. It will either help me through this latest crisis phase, or be such a terrible reminder of my continuing failure that I'll have to smash it into atomic bits and lose myself in some mosh pit instead, and dance like a primal being incapable of communicating my overwhelming emotions by any other means.

Yasmine would understand what I mean. She used to get me out of my occasional funks by giving me a look. *You're bedeviling me,* I'd tell her. *You're a Yasmanian devil.* She'd laugh with a gypsy whoop, and climb on top of me, and her whirling dervish of kisses would drive me to the brink of insanity, then reel me back in to the safety of her cradling arms.

People are drifting back inside the theater. Beyond the story-high windows, Ann's still yapping on her cell phone. I go outside and tell her, without waiting for a pause in the conversation, *we need to get back to our seats.* She rolls her eyes, tells whoever she's talking to she'll call back soon, and flicks off the phone.

Do we have to go back in? she asks.

I really like them. And I paid a lot of money for these tickets.

Ann understands money; she speaks fluent currency. It's her measure of success, of people's worth – even her own.

Okay, she says, but stamps her foot a little.

I walk. *Let's get back before the lights go down.*

We just make it, stumbling past those seated in our aisle. I'm apologizing to the woman next to my seat for stepping on her foot when my eyes snap to Yasmine's. Her eyes are wide, watching me. I freeze.

The lights go out.

I fall into my seat, riveted to her through the darkness. When the stage lights come up, I see only her profile as she watches the musicians take their places. She's blinking too rapidly, though – a sign she's nervous. She glances at me, jumps a little when she sees me, like I've slapped her. I feel like my brain's out of order, my movements are in slow motion. I can't think of anything else to do but stare.

Her companion leans his head toward hers, says something. She turns back to the stage.

The guitarist plays with such intensity of feeling, I close my eyes as the song sends me out of my body, floating on the waves of music. I imagine myself with Yasmine, on our last good day together. It had rained all day, and we'd stayed in bed, exploring each other like two spelunkers, exhilarating at new discoveries. I replayed as much as I could remember of that day in my head.

Are you all right? Ann whispers harshly into my ear.

I crash again, angry at the abrupt landing. *Sshhhh!*

You're weird, she says.

I close my eyes again, trying to recapture the moment. But it's irretrievable, and now the song is ending, and fury builds inside me.

I quell my anger with this thought: I'll drop her off at home tonight, and never call her again.

I reopen my eyes as the trio begins a new song, and see Yasmine, watching me again. She looks sad. Her sadness creates a new chasm inside me, spilling her sadness into mine.

I miss you, I mouth at her.

She looks away. Then looks back.

I miss you, I mouth again, more insistently.

She looks from me to Ann, who's now leaning forward, suddenly attentive. But I can't stop looking at Yasmine. I tilt my head toward the door, my eyebrows raised as if to say *please.*

She looks uncertain, but doesn't say no.

I tilt my head again.

Are you flirting with that girl? Ann says.

My eyes beg Yasmine: *please please please please please.*

To my astonishment, she gets up, says something quick to her companion, and walks up the aisle, her eyes shining in the near-darkness, locked on mine. As if I'd taken a hit of helium, I stand.

No, I tell Ann. *I'm leaving with her.*

Laughter bubbles inside me for the first time in weeks, and I hurry toward Yasmine, whisper a general *sorry* for the missteps landing on others' feet, for the weeks I've wasted alone, for trying to fill the chasm Yasmine left with a shallow puddle named Ann.

I grasp her hand and we walk through the exit. I feel my feet more solidly on the ground even as we're practically waltzing, as I ask Yasmine, *Can we go somewhere and talk?*

She stops, then, lays a hand on my cheek, like a blind woman divining the true person underneath.

Yes, she says finally.

The pianist, bassist and guitarist provide the soundtrack to this moment I could live in forever. I kiss her, capture her in my arms for a short time, in defiance of the song that's ending and the starry sky destined to dissipate into morning.

C.A. Masterson calls Pennsylvania home, but she'll always be a Jersey girl at heart. When not with her family, she's in her lair, concocting a magical brew of contemporary, historical, and fantasy/paranormal stories. Also writing as Cate Masters, look for her at catemasters.blogspot.com, and in far-flung corners of the web.

The Mirror

By
Susan E. Bangs

Madeline waited patiently for her train. It had been a long week and she wanted to get out of the city. The other passengers stood on the platform, some anxiously looking at their watches. Finally, her train arrived and she got into the second car that had several available seats. She situated herself comfortably and waited for the train to lurch forward. As she waited, she fumbled in her purse for the ticket she had purchased. The conductor began his rounds as the train slowly left the station.

Accidentally, Madeline knocked her purse onto the floor and in picking up the items that had fallen out, she noticed an envelope discarded under the seat in front of her. It was a large manila one that had "Open If Found" written in bold letters on the outside.

Curious, but hesitant, Madeline opened the envelope and found a mirror inside. When she looked at herself in it, a stranger looked back. Suddenly the stranger spoke, "Congratulations Madeline, you have found what many have sought. Think carefully before you speak because the first three wishes that escape your lips will be yours."

Madeline thought she had fallen asleep and was dreaming, but when she looked again at the mirror, the same face looked back at her. "Who are you and what kind of wishes can I make?"

"I am who you want me to be and your wishes can be anything."

"I want to be with you wherever it is that you are."

"That's simple enough. Come along then."

The next thing she knew, Madeline was transported to a beautiful, plush landscape where the air was fresh and everything around her burst with color.

"Oh, I haven't felt this alive in a while!" she exclaimed.

"What else do you desire?" the stranger asked.

"I want to be in an evening gown dancing with the most handsome man there."

"Done then," the mirror said.

Madeline could hear the music and felt herself swirling to a Viennese waltz. She was captivated by the charming man whose arm encircled her waist as they effortlessly glided around the room.

"You have one final wish," the stranger said.

"I'm so tired of my mundane routine—I want to leave it forever."

"Done then," the mirror replied.

When Madeline's son arrived to pick his mother up for dinner, he found her in her usual folding chair, where she always waited, holding a mirror smiling and slightly slumped over. The son tried to wake her, but couldn't. He felt a sudden sense of grief yet peace overwhelming him. His mother's battle with dementia was over.

"Done then," he said as he gently bent to kiss her good-bye.

Susan E. Bangs is a professor at Harrisburg Area Community College where she teaches English as a Second Language and Spanish.

BETSY'S DELIGHT

BY
MARLENE ROSS

"Let's go for ice cream, Hon. What do you think, Dan?"
Betsy leans into the doorway of her husband's home office.
"It's so hot. How about it? Hon, did you hear me? Want
some ice cream?"

"I have to finish this report," says Dan, closely
scrutinizing the figures on his laptop, "and I have a
conference call in about ten minutes."

"Can't you take a break from work? It's Saturday for
Pete's sake; didn't you hear the news bulletin? If every
household reduced power consumption by five percent, a
shortage might be avoided during this heat wave. Turn off
your computer and help out."

"Not if I want to keep my job, Bets. We're bidding on a
huge contract and I need this report done on time for the
call. . .which will come in a few minutes."

"What about after the conference call? Can we go
then?" Betsy gently massages Dan's neck and shoulders,
humming the jingle advertising of the Delightful Ice Cream
Store. She notices more grey in his black hair, especially
at the temples and a few more wrinkles around his laugh
lines. "Maybe then. Please, hon? I'd really like a cool
strawberry ice cream. Mmm. . .delightful. . .just like their
ads say. You could use a break too."

"Where is this place, Bets?" Dan concentrates on his
computer screen. "Don't we have ice cream in the freezer?"

"Sure, but it's not home made with fresh fruit." Betsy
waves her hand in the air for effect. "Not the same at all."

"I want to try this new place I told you about:
'Delightful Ice Cream.'It just opened up downtown. They
make homemade ice cream using fresh fruits named
'Delightful Strawberry Cream', 'Delightful Pineapple

Passion', 'Delightful Cheery Cherry', 'Delightful Blueberry Burst', 'Delightful Choc full O Chocolate'," Betsy says.

"Bets, you could be their marketing director, reciting all the ice cream flavors and humming their catchy jingle." Just then Dan's expression changes from annoyance to reluctant persuasion.

"OK," Dan surrenders. "It's the ice cream store immediately after the conference call. You've convinced me but what about parking? Do they have a parking lot?" He stalls again for more time, eyes glued to the screen.

Betsy brightens. "I don't think so, but we may get lucky and find a spot."

"Mmm. Downtown is pretty sparse for parking. I remember the last time I went down to the new hardware store, I ended up driving around for ten minutes waiting for someone to leave and then the space was on the other side of the street. Crossing was a pain in the neck— and dangerous."

"Oh, we'll manage. I'll tell the kids; we'll be ready in ten minutes."

"You better make it twenty minutes, these calls usually run longer than intended," Dan says, but Betsy was already around the corner and springing up the stairs.

"Tracy, Connor, Shelly! Get ready! We're going for ice cream at the new place downtown!" Betsy rushes down the hall.

"Can't go," shouts Connor, "going to shoot hoops. The guys will be here in a few to pick me up."

"Oh, can't you go a bit later? I want all of us to try this new place together; like a family outing."

"Ah, Mom, I'm too old for that stuff." Connor dismisses the idea, hands on his hips and his almost six foot frame blocking the doorway.

"You're just fifteen and age shouldn't interfere with family togetherness," remarks Betsy. "Come on, Connor," she cajoles at the same time playfully cuffing his left arm and giving him a hug. He's getting so tall and broad; she could barely reach his cheek for a kiss. "Wouldn't you enjoy a nice cool refreshing ice cream, especially today?"

"Can I get the Delightful Razberry Razy?" exclaims a smiling curly blonde Shelly, skipping down the hall towards them, her blue eyes dancing. "My friend Marsha got one last week and she said it was super!" Shelly twirls around in place, squealing and jumping up and down.

"Sure can, kiddo." Betsy leans down to hug her agreeable eight-year-old. "Anything you want; and your big brother can, too!" Shelly squeals in delight and jumps up on Connor for a piggyback ride. They jog down the hall and out into the back yard, Betsy beaming with maternal pride. Connor is really growing up. Soon he'll be off to college and on his own. Shelly is so young and innocent, such a joy. Betsy realized how much she misses those precious moments with her family, the togetherness.

She shouts at her oldest daughter's bedroom door, "Tracy, did you hear? We're going for ice cream to the new place that just opened up. Tracy, honey, get ready."

"Not now, Mom, Margie is going to call me. She just got these new neighbors and they have a son who is really hot! I can't wait to hear all about him. Besides, ice cream is too fattening, especially the home made kind. They use whole milk, and sugar and too many calories. I just can't eat that stuff, Mom, if I want to fit into my jeans."

"But it's OK once in a while," consoles Betsy. "Don't you want to cool off with a Delightful Pretty Peachy or Banana Beauty? I'm sure they have low cal. Besides, you have no worries, sweetheart, you look fine in your jeans."

"Mom... I told you! NO!"

"But I thought the whole family would go. It's kind of a special treat. Not much fun if we're all not there to enjoy it," she pleads, hoping her thirteen year old will change her mind.

"MOM! Stop nagging me! Their ice cream has about a gazillion calories!"

Betsy shrugs in disappointment. Ever since Tracy turned thirteen, she seems so rebellious and irritated. Do all teenagers turn down an offer of home made ice cream? How things have changed. . .oh well, at least Shelly is all for it.

After brushing her hair and stepping gingerly into her new sandals, Betsy yells over her shoulder to Shelly, standing in the doorway. "Want to see if your Dad's ready?"

"Sure Mom," exclaims Betsy's dutiful little daughter. Smiling widely towards her mother and with her task at hand, she rushes down the hall, her blond pony tail bobbing.

Shelly returns in two breathless minutes and blurts out: "Dad said, 'ten minutes' 'n' meet him in the car with the air conditioning running."

"OK, sweetie, let's get some cool water for the dog and I'll turn off the TV and computer in case that storm comes. After three full days and nights of temperatures near a hundred degrees, we may get that storm they're predicting. I hope so. . .it is too hot."

"I'll close the umbrella and bring in the cushions while I'm out here on the patio," yells Connor, dribbling the basketball for a neat lay up against the backboard.

"Don't forget to put the dog inside before he jumps in the car; you know how carsick he gets."

"Come on Sherlock, in you go." Connor wrestles the dog inside and locks the door securely. "All done Mom."

In the car, Betsy starts the motor and turns on the air conditioning to full blast. She and Shelly sing along with KC and the Sunshine Band playing "That's the way, ahah, ahah, I like it, ahah, ahah." She imagines a mouthful of smooth strawberry and Shelly pretends to squash some sweet raspberries in her mouth. They clap a high five and smile at each other in anticipation.

Dan finally joins them and raises his eyebrows at Betsy. "It's only Shelly going?" Betsy just smiles and shakes her head. Slowly they back down the driveway, finally on their way.

At the bottom of the curb, Shelly notices Tracy running to catch up, cell phone at her ear. Hopping in the back seat, she explains, "Connor's coming too. You can drop him off at the basketball court on the way back. He thought a jolt of ice cream would help his game. I can talk to Margie on my cell and I might get frozen yogurt."

Betsy smiles, contently. They are all together for this treat. Dan starts singing; "I scream, you scream, we all scream for ICE CREAM!" Everyone joins in. Finally, they are getting into a convivial mood. Betsy sits back, pleased. This will be a fine family outing.

Half way to their destination, stopped at a traffic light, Dan says, "Wait a minute, Betsy, did you bring your wallet? Mine's in my other pants."

"What? You must be kidding. My purse is at home on the dining room table!" Betsy gives Dan a sidelong looks-could-kill grimace. A quick check of the compartments and console offer no help. Looking doubtfully towards Connor and Tracy, Betsy asks, "Any of you have money?"

Tracy holds her hands up. "Don't look at me Mom, my allowance for the next two months is gone!"

Conner says flatly, "I'm broke."

Shelly has two nickels, a dime and four pennies in her back pocket, including some white lint.

Dan says with authority, "We'll just turn around, it won't take long."

Conner groans, "The guys will be waiting."

"What if Margie calls?" Tracy fusses, "I can't talk in here!"

Connor snaps, "You guys talk nonsense anyway. You won't miss much."

"Mom, make him stop. He's always nasty to me and my friends," blurts Tracy on the verge of tears, punching Connor's shoulder trying to stop him from messing her hair. Tracy shrieks and tries to push Connor away. Meanwhile, Shelly is caught in the middle of this fight and yells to them, "Behave!"

Dan commands, "Knock it off, you two! Five minutes. That's all it will take." Now, on a mission, Dan makes a U turn at the corner to race back home.

Back at the house, Betsy scrambles past the dog, bumps her shin in the doorway and hastily retrieves her purse. They were back on their way in no time, a subdued Connor and Tracy grumbling in the back seat, sitting with their arms folded and staring through their windows. Shelly tries to keep the peace by telling Connor that he might like a Delightful Monster at the Delight. Marsha's brother got one and said it was awesome. It had chocolate ice cream and nuts with blackberries and lots of chocolate bits. Connor chuckles and ruffles Shelly's hair in a playful mood.

"Here we are. . .and look, a parking space right out front.   I told you we might get lucky," exclaims Betsy, smiling toward Dan. Everyone scrambles out of the car.

Connor runs ahead up the stairs to open the front door. "It must be stuck," complains Connor. Dan muscles his way to the handle.

"You're right, it won't open," says Dan, trying to shake loose the lock. "Knock on the door, that'll get someone's attention," he asserts, moving closer to have a look inside. "Hey! No one's in there!"

"Oh no," cries a dejected Betsy, pointing to a hand written card, in bold black letters: Closed Due to Power Outage. "I guess the heat wave did cause the power outage they predicted. Dan stamps his foot on the top step, shouting, "Darn, I was so ready for a homemade ice cream."

Betsy pats his arm. "I know, honey, so am I. That strawberry delight was almost right on the tip of my tongue." They all look longingly at the doily covered round tables with white chairs and the gleaming polished white counter. Shelly breaks into choking sobs, large teardrops falling down her cheeks. Betsy puts her arm around the slender shoulders of this disappointed little one and hugs her gently.

Heavy dark clouds move in and the brisk wind whips up around them. With heads hanging, the entire family descends the steps and crunches back into the hot car. Hoping to lighten the mood, Dan suggests, "Well, we can always come tomorrow. I want that Blueberry Burst," he says, smiling at Betsy.

"They're not open Sunday!" Betsy snaps through clenched teeth. "It's DOWNTOWN! Everything downtown is closed on Sundays, Danny Boy!" She leans towards Dan's face, folding her arms tightly over her chest.

"Like," Dan waves his hands in dismay above the steering wheel, "I'm supposed to know about downtown, Bets!"

"Well, you knew about the hardware store, didn't you?"

"That's different!"

Rolling her eyes, Betsy sneers, "Oh, yeah? What's so different about it, huh? You tell me. I'm waiting!"

151

Connor slinks down into his seat, adjusts his ear buds, and turns up the volume on his IPOD.

Tracy yells, "Mom, I can't get Margie on the phone!"

Shelly begins to whimper, "I gotta go to the bathroom!"

"Don't worry honey, we'll be home soon," sooths Dan with great sympathy for his sweet little girl.

"Maybe we can come next weekend, next Saturday," chirps Dan, still trying.

"I'll be away at my mother's, helping her move, remember," spits Betsy.

"I'm going with Margie's family to their cottage," announces Tracy. "And Connor's got basketball camp."

Shelly will be at a birthday party all day. Betsy's heart sank.

"If you hadn't taken so long with that conference call," Betsy stews.

"Yeah, and who forgot her purse?" Dan yells; angry at being blamed. "Is it my fault the dang store closed?" Dan pounds the steering wheel for emphasis.

"Keep your voice down," yells Betsy. "We're all upset enough already." Turning her head towards the side window, Betsy stares ahead, smoldering inside. This always happens when I plan a perfectly happy family outing; why do I bother?

They drive along in silence. Large raindrops begin to hit the windshield, increasing in volume, dark clouds roiling overhead. Thunder could be heard rumbling in the distance. The heat wave was finally broken and this storm would bring welcome relief.

"Good thing we brought in the patio furniture," Shelly says, trying to be cheerful. Staring out of the windows, everyone is lost in their own thoughts, watching the storm clouds darken.

"What a waste of time, I didn't want to come in the first place. Thanks for nothing, Mom and now my phone won't work."

"You never recharge that phone! No wonder it doesn't work," Betsy says.

Connor rolls his eyes. "Here we go again."

Betsy scolds him, "Connor, stay out of it! This doesn't concern you!"

"What did I do?" He turns to Tracy and smacks the back of her head. "Thanks a lot Traceee! Mom's mad at me, now!"

"Mom," cries Tracy, "make him stop!" Just then a bolt of lightning cracks loudly and thunder rumbles. Shelly holds her ears, frightful of the storm. Tracy wraps her arms around her trembling shoulders and Connor pats her head gently and rubs her back.

As soon as Dan parks in the driveway, everyone scrambles into the house trying to avoid the downpour. Dan and Connor head directly to the den to watch a game, Tracy runs to the bathroom to blow dry her hair and Shelly plays her iPOD, silently singing to some tune. Betsy sinks down into the living room sofa and exhales a long sigh.

Rivulets of rain stream down the picture window and the sky grows even darker. Connor passes Betsy in the hall with a bag of chips and a can of coke and comments "Don't worry about dinner, Mom. Dad and I will get pizza as soon as the rain stops." Betsy shakes her head "OK" with closed eyes. It's just like a man to think pizza and a bag of chips will make everything all right. Naturally, Dan would think of his stomach. The storm doesn't help either. Her bruised ankle starts to throb. Lightning illuminates the sky and more rain pours down. Would it ever end? Police sirens and fire trucks scream in the distance.

Tracy yells down the steps, a towel wrapped around her head. "Hey, Mom, I just talked to Margie and guess what she said? You know the new family who moved in next door?"

"Sure," Betsy says then she whispers to herself, "The one with the son who's so hot?"

Tracy continues, "Well, the power went out at their place and they are looking for people to take stuff. Guess what store they own, Mom? Guess! Come on!"

Betsy is in no mood for guessing games. Everything is back to the same old thing. Dan's on his computer, again. Connor's watching some game, again. Shelly's on her iPOD, again, listening to music with her dolls again and Tracy's in the bathroom and on the phone, AGAIN.

Now Tracy wants to annoy her. "Mom, guess!"

153

Betsy agrees to play along and mutters to herself, "The hardware store?" She shouts towards Tracy upstairs, "The cell phone recharging store? The 'don't worry about my feelings' store? The 'family that doesn't do anything happy together' store?"

"No. Mom! "It's that 'stuff your family into a hot car, forget your purse, turn around and go back, closed on Sunday ice cream store!"

Betsy's eyes brighten, "Do you mean it's the Delightful Homemade Ice Cream Store?"

"That's what I've been trying to tell you mom!"

"Will they have Razberry Razy?" Shelly races from her room, running down the stairs and leaping onto the sofa near her mom. Betsy fumbles for her sandals and jumps up to get the car keys. "Let's go find out, my delightful little one."

Marlene Ross has been the director of New Cumberland Library's Write On group for the past twelve years. She studied Psychology and the Humanities and has traveled extensively in the United States and several countries. She lives in New Cumberland and loves to brag about her six accomplished, talented and very special grandchildren.

MOVING TARGETS

BY
DEBRA A. VARSANYI

Her hands clenched into tight fists as Sarah peered through her apartment window. She watched Nazi soldiers kick a Jewish man and wrap a rope around his waist. Onlookers hollered, "Dirty Jew!" *It's getting worse every day. Will the hatred ever stop?*

She flinched when her husband, Richard, touched her cheek. He turned her towards him and brushed her dark curls from her forehead. Worry furrowed her brow.

"Honey, don't watch," he said, "I'll always love and protect you."

"What if they arrest us? Richard, I want to go to America today! I wish we weren't in Vienna."

"Sarah, I'm securing tickets for us. I met with an associate, Joshua, who helps hide and relocate Jews. "

"I know...you're doing what you can. But, did you hear the news? The Nazi's Party decreed Jews must wear yellow Star of David arm bands by next month...we'll be Moving Targets."

"Yes, I heard. I wish they would leave us alone. Oh! I almost forgot, my mama's downstairs waiting for me to bring up her belongings."

Sarah groaned.

A few minutes later, Esther swung the apartment door open, bustled in and set her purse on the pink Victorian chair that sat resting opposite a brown settee. She settled her small pudgy body into the settee and surveyed the room with impatient eyes.

"Where's Sarah?" Esther said, banging her cane on the wooden floor.

Sarah came out of the kitchen, wiping her hands on her apron. "Excuse me, Esther; I'm preparing a special supper for you."

155

"You're excused. Go back to the kitchen and my son and I will chat."

"Mama!" Richard yelled.

"You don't want the food to burn, dear," Esther said.

Sarah escaped to the warm kitchen. She grabbed a lemon from a bowl, cut it in half, and squeezed it in her hand over a water pitcher, while thinking: *I'll never be good enough for my mother-in-law. How am I going to make this work?* She looked upward and prayed, "God, give me strength and patience."

After supper they rested in the parlor and listened to the shortwave receiver. As they tuned in to an American station, Bob Hope sang, "Thanks for the Memories." Sarah bit her lip when she heard: "News update: The Nazi's burned synagogues and ransacked Jewish businesses today, November 9, 1938." Sarah shuddered. Richard shut the receiver off and drew her close.

"I brought something to display," Esther said. She dug in her bag, pulled out a picture, and placed it on the coffee table. "I brought our family portrait from your wedding."

Excuse me, "I'm tired," Sarah said and hurried from the room.

"Goodnight, Mom," Richard said and rushed after Sarah.

Keeping her voice low so Esther won't hear she said, "Richard, can you believe it? I'll never forget. We were about to have our wedding picture taken and your mom asked me to get something from her purse. Then she convinced the photographer to flash the picture without me, and told me I was tardy. I wish you'd never given her the picture."

"Honey, I'm sorry, I can't change her. She isn't well enough to be alone. Let's talk about America instead," Richard suggested. "Esther will live with my sister, Mary, once we're in America."

"That's a relief," Sarah said. "I can picture America now, a place where I don't have to be afraid of who I am."

"Yes, a land where freedom exists. Sarah I'm tired... let's go to sleep," he said.

Tuesday morning Richard took forever to get ready for work.

"Richard, what's wrong?" Sarah asked. "You should have left an hour ago."

"The Nazi's set fire to the shoe factory yesterday and arrested Seth, the owner. I'm unemployed."

"Why didn't you tell me? How can we get to America now? I'm going to be sick," she said and ran for the bathroom. Richard followed her.

"Honey ... you all right? You've been so upset; I didn't want to tell you." He handed her a towel and noticed Esther heading towards them. "I have to leave. I don't want mama to know."

Esther peeked in the bathroom and said, "Richard, shouldn't you be at work?"

"Sarah's sick."

"Go, Richard, I'll watch over her." Esther patted Sarah on the back, "Let it go honey, you'll feel better when it's gone. I'll make you some hot water with lemon juice — it fixes everything."

Later in the day, Sarah and Esther rested at the kitchen table, while they snacked on grapes. Hearing the front door slam, Sarah hurried to greet her husband. He was breathing hard. "Are you okay?"

"I'm fine Sarah; I need to catch my breath. I think I ran up the steps too fast. How are you, honey? Feeling better?"

"I'm just a little tired."

After a light supper of gefilte fish and bread they retired to the parlor.

The next morning announced itself with a rumbling thunderstorm. Sarah not only heard it, but felt her stomach accompanying the storm. She ran from the bed and vomited.

As she lost the last of her supper, Esther banged on the bathroom door. Sarah clutched her stomach and opened the door. The old woman loomed above her, hands on her hips. "You done yet, I can't hold it so long."

She lay back in bed and snuggled next to Richard. In the morning, she reached for him and found only a clump of blankets. Sarah glanced at the clock: 12:30. She ambled out to the kitchen where Esther sat at the wooden table knitting.

"It's about time you joined the living," Esther said.

"I'm not in the mood. . .oh! Forget it."

"Did you have your flow this month?"

Sarah's water glass slipped from her hand and smashed on the wooden floor.

Esther shouted, "I did not think so...you're pregnant, Sarah. I'm gonna be a grandmother!"

Sarah dropped into the nearest chair, her mouth hung open. "I've been so occupied with the possibility of war...I lost track. It's been two months, Esther. What am I going to do?"

Esther squeezed her hand, "You don't have to do anything. The baby will come...let's see...July. Don't worry, I'll be here to direct you."

"Esther, excuse me, I need a moment."

Sarah paced in her bedroom. *"God, how can I handle all this?"* After facing the truth, she placed her hand on her stomach and thanked God for His gift, a child. The afternoon passed by while Esther and Sarah cleaned the apartment.

Richard entered the kitchen and kissed Sarah. "What smells wonderful?"

"Wiener schnitzel."

"Mama said you have good news for me."

"I wanted to tell you when I'm ready," she said, throwing a dish towel on the table.

"Come Sarah, let's have it."

"I'm pregnant."

He dragged his fingers through his hair and gawked at her.

"Richard, say something?" She twisted the hem of her apron.

"I can't believe it! A baby?" He placed his hand on her stomach and looked into her brown eyes and said, "You made me a happy man."

"You're not upset?"

"Sarah, I love you, and God will help us find a way. I may have a new position. Head shoe designer by Friday."

Esther banged on the kitchen door and said, "Aren't we gonna celebrate this occasion together?"

"We'll be there in a minute, Mama," Richard answered.

Cold meat and bread was placed on the coffee table for dinner. Sarah reached into the pantry and grabbed their last bag of figs to celebrate. They spent the evening discussing the child to come.

Wednesday morning the bell rang and rang. "Richard, unwind it ...it's piercing my ears." She reached past her husband and snatched up the alarm. "Richard, wake up!" He didn't respond. She touched his face. It was ice cold. Sarah listened for a heart beat! She screamed and pleaded, "Richard...You can't leave me!" Her body convulsed while tears cascaded down her cheeks.

Esther burst in the door. "What's wrong? You screamed loud enough to wake the dead."

"He's dead...Richard's dead? Oh! God, help me!"

Pushing Sarah away, Esther shook her son and hollered, "Get up, Richard. I'm telling you – you should get up! I'll call the doctor and he'll make him better." She left the room.

Sarah sat in the bed beside her husband's still body. She wept rocking back and forth.

Esther walked into the bedroom. "There are no doctors." She knelt beside the bed, touched his hand, and wailed, "My son...my son."

Sarah placed her trembling hand on Esther's back and said, "I'll call the Rabbi."

She sunk into the settee waiting for the Rabbi. *I'm all alone now.*

The Rabbi arrived with men who prepared her husband's body for burial.

"We need to bury him, Sarah," the Rabbi said.

"How am I going to live without him?" Sarah asked sobbing.

The Rabbi placed his hand on her shoulder and said, "God will provide. It's time ladies, follow behind us."

The heaviness weighed on Sarah's soul as she trudged through the mud laden streets. Reaching the cemetery she cried as she watched the men lower her husband's wooden casket into the ground. After the ceremony, she picked up a rock and set it on his grave and said, "Tell me why Richard?" and left.

One week after Richard's heart attack, Sarah sat in the parlor wringing a handkerchief. *I'm stuck in Austria...my child won't know freedom. What will become of us?* A knock on the door startled her. Opening the door, she found an envelope with her name on it. She tore it open and read. "Meet me at the bakery, noon tomorrow. I'm an associate of your husband-Joshua." Sarah's hand shook. Esther stood behind her. "What is it?"

"A note...read it."

"What are you going to do?"

"I'm not sure."

"Well, I'm sure of one thing," Esther said, "We need to leave for the outdoor market if we plan on eating."

Sarah stepped around the broken glass from the Jewish businesses. She buried her clenched fists in her pockets as she passed one propaganda poster after another plastered on the brick buildings.

She reached for a potato from a market stand. A Nazi solider blocked her reach and stood ogling her. Her cheek twitched and she said, "Excuse me." He didn't move. Esther stood in front of Sarah like a bear protecting her cub. "Show some respect. You can see by our clothes we're grieving," she said.

The Nazi's eyebrow cocked upward, and he moved aside. "Let it be known, we Germans show respect."

At home again, she faced Esther and said, "Thank you for helping me. I thought you didn't like me."

"Oh! No, dear, I love you. I just didn't want to share my son. He's all I had after my husband died. But don't worry, Sarah, I'm taking care of you now.

The next day, Sarah, sat across from Esther at the kitchen table sipping a cup of tea. "Esther, I don't know how, but we're going to America. My baby's going to know freedom. I've decided to meet the man who left the note."

"Do you think that's wise?"

"Yes, if he's a Nazi, he would have already bashed the door in and dragged us off."

"I'm coming with you."

"I'd rather go alone; it would be faster...if I have to run."

Sarah wore Esther's coat and hat, hoping to escape being noticed by the Germans. She paused in front of the bakery and tried to blend in. Then she heard a man's voice. "Gruss dich, Sarah." She started to turn around, but the man said, "Don't! Keep looking in the window. I promised your husband if something ever happened to him, I would personally hand you this. "Go, Sarah," he said and moved away. She stuffed the envelope inside her coat and rushed home.

Once inside the house, she locked the door and ripped open the envelope. Her fingers trembled. She stared unbelieving at its contents. Then she whispered, "Richard, thank you. I wish you could come with us."

Sarah hurried to Esther's bedroom. "Esther, I have wonderful news." She found her lying on the floor. Rushing to her side, she knelt on the floor beside her.

"I think it's a stroke. My right leg and arm are so numb."

Sarah helped her into a sitting position. "How can I help?"

"Get my medicine from my purse." She gulped her pill and said, "Tell me the news."

"Esther, look... three tickets and a map to cross the border. We're going to America."

"I don't think I'm going, but you must for the baby."

"I'm not leaving you behind. I'll find a way."

A few days later Sarah said, "Esther, we need to leave for Hungary tonight. The Nazi's started arresting Jews."

"I can't. I'm dragging my left leg. I'll slow you down."

"Esther, look at me, you're going to lean on me. We're making this journey together. My child needs a grandmother."

Sarah left the room to begin packing.

At dusk she said, "Esther, it's now or never. We can do this." Tying two strips of material, she tied one around Esther's right thigh and one around her left thigh. Then she wrapped the other strip around their calves. "Let's practice walking in the apartment. I'll step forward and your right leg will follow mine."

"Your idea works," she said.

"Esther, we need to hurry."

They hobbled down the apartment steps together, and slid into an alley avoiding the Nazi's.

As they entered the forest, branches from tall spruce trees reached out and obstructed their path. Each step crunched from fallen pinecones and leaves. A relentless headwind pushed against them.

"Sarah, it's dark. Light the torch."

"I will, Esther, but I'll keep it low to the ground. We don't want the Nazi's finding us."

"I must rest. We've walked for hours."

"All right ... but only for a short time. We have to cross east into the border to Hungary before morning. Let's sit against this tree."

A cool mist swirled along the forest floor as they rested. They huddled close together for warmth.

Sarah closed her eyes and prayed, *God, please help us.* Falling asleep under the starry sky, she awoke to a sound of a twig breaking. Goose bumps covered her entire body. She held her breath. Something was moving near to them while Esther snored on in oblivion.

It fell over their legs.

Sarah tried to get up, but her leg was still tied to Esther's. A lantern was lit, and a man squatted in front of them and said, "Don't be afraid, I won't hurt you."

Esther awoke and swung at him, punching him in the jaw, "Run, Sarah, Run!"

"Esther, what have you done?"

The large man with dark hair put his hat back on and rubbed his reddened cheek. "You throw a good punch, ma'am," he said.

"Who are you? What are you doing here?" She asked.

"First things first, my name is Isaac, and I'm on my way to Hungary."

"Nice to meet you, Isaac, but we need to get moving, Esther," Sarah said.

"Where are you headed?" Isaac asked.

"Hungary. And then to America," Sarah replied while rubbing her hands together.

"I envy you both, America. May we travel together?" Isaac inquired.

"If you wish," Sarah said.

They set off with the two women still bound together.

After a while, Isaac said, "Ladies, may I help?" He handed a large sturdy stick to Esther, and said "Lean on me." Sarah untied the strips. Several hours passed and the pale light of the sunrise began to envelop the forest. They left the barren woods behind and walked through fields of trampled wheat.

"Shh, Nazis, get down!" Sarah whispered.

"I can't believe it....we're only fifty feet from the border," Isaac said.

"We have to run for it?" Sarah asked.

"I don't see another choice," Isaac answered.

"Are you serious?" Esther whined.

Isaac picked up Esther as if she was a sack of potatoes and plunged ahead. Sarah ran to keep up with them.

"Jews!" A Nazi shouted and charged after them.

Breathless, they crossed the border into Hungary as a shot rang out.

"Sarah tumbled forward and screamed, "I'm shot!"

Isaac bent down and lifted her in his arms. Esther followed using her stick and dragging her leg.

He set Sarah down on the dried grass. Blood soaked through her coat at her upper arm. Esther hobbled to Sarah and removed her jacket. Isaac tore the sleeve of her dress to find the source of the bleeding. Sarah lay still on the ground.

Esther wailed. "Help her! She's pregnant."

It's only a flesh wound, Esther. Sarah's will be fine." He ripped a piece of his shirt off to tie around her wound. "We're across. We're safe now."

Sarah leaned against him.

"Thank you, Isaac," she said. Isaac stood and looked around.

"Look, Sarah," he said. "The airport is just ahead ... your ticket to America.

She smiled through the pain. "Isaac, are you ready for an adventure?

"An adventure?"

"Yes, I have an extra ticket to America."

Debra A. Varsanyi is a graduate of the Institute of Children's Literature and attended writing classes at Elizabethtown College and Harrisburg Area Community College. She actively participates in workshops at the Cleve J. Fredricksen Library. Debra and her husband, Gabe, reside in Pennsylvania with their dog, Tebah.

CREATURE OF HABIT

BY
DON HELIN

The growl of a truck engine and the rumble of mufflers split the early-morning air. My sweaty hands slipped on the shovel as I struggled to fill in the hole. I patted the dirt level and smoothed it out.

A door slammed. I broke for the edge of the woods and threw myself under a white pine. Too late I realized I'd left the shovel laying on the ground.

The sun peeked above the tree line, gray shadows stretching toward me like fingers of a hand. Jake stalked around the corner of the trailer, not fifteen feet from where I hid. Staring first at the shovel, then the patch of dirt, he picked up the shovel and stomped on the dirt with his work boots.

I didn't dare breathe, sure he'd walk over to the tree line and see me. My mouth ran dry and sweat stung my eyes.

Jake leaned the shovel against the trailer and started around toward the front, glancing back once more. The door to his trailer banged shut, shattering the silence. A great horned owl hooted its final morning call.

I sucked in air and did a low crawl deeper into the woods. Multiflora rose thorns ripped at my bare arms and legs as I stood and ran.

Later that day at our local coffee shop, John Williamson, a Pennsylvania State Trooper and fellow veteran, entered and poured a cup.

He pulled off his hat, hitched up his pistol belt, and sat. "How ya been, Percy?"

"Been better. Something's bothering me."

He poured sugar into his coffee. "Can I help?"

"Maybe. You know, I'm a creature of habit. That's what caused this whole mess."

"You are that." He laughed. "What mess?"

"Well, every morning I drag my raggedy-assed body out of bed and go for a jog. If I didn't, this six-foot frame wouldn't stay at 190 very long."

He tapped his gut. "No kidding."

I leaned forward. "About three months ago, a young couple moved into a trailer at the turn-around of my run. Over the next month, I watched them haul away all kinds of paint cans, batteries, a stack of tires, barrels, and you know, assorted junk. They even painted the trailer and got rid of a beat-up Ford Mustang on blocks."

"Uh huh."

"I'd see a woman of about thirty working in the yard. Cute lady with a blond ponytail, wearing a Penn State sweatshirt. She'd wave and smile at me."

Williamson waited.

"One morning, I walked over and welcomed her to the neighborhood. She told me her name was Molly and her husband's Jake."

He watched me over the lip of his cup. "You seem to have taken a liking to her."

"Yeah. I mean no. Then I asked her about a bruise under her left eye. Her grin disappeared and she glanced up at the trailer. Told me I'd better go. When I turned to start down the road, a man appeared in the doorway."

Williamson put his cup down. "What'd he look like?"

"Big—filled the doorway—black hair and a bushy beard. He wore jeans and a red checkered shirt. Anyway, over the next couple of weeks, I'd spot her out in the yard, washing their truck . . . ."

"Was she wearing a bathing suit?"

"Bikini. She looked good." Williamson was sharp. "I'd see her working in the garden. I'd wave and she'd wave back."

"Where's this trailer?"

"Up Smith Road, about half way to the Y with Valley Road. But then, I didn't see her outside anymore. The flowers she'd planted wilted."

He pulled a pen out of his pocket.

"This morning I went jogging like always. When I reached the trailer, his truck was gone. I stopped to stretch. Well, my curiosity won out. I walked up to the trailer and knocked. No answer. I figured it wouldn't hurt to look around a little."

"God dammit, Percy, that's trespassing."

"Let me finish. I was about to leave when I spotted a patch of fresh dirt."

He put down his coffee. "How big?"

"Maybe two feet by five feet."

I had him interested. "A shovel leaned against the trailer. As I poked around in the dirt, a truck pulled up."

"He caught you?"

I shook my head. "I dropped the shovel and ran like hell, but he knew someone had been there."

Williamson pulled on his graying mustache. "I can see why you're concerned. I'll drive by." He put down his cup and pointed his finger at me. "I don't care if your curiosity is killing you. Leave this alone."

The next morning, I got the surprise of my life when a woman stood in front of the trailer washing a black Pontiac. I walked over. She could have been Molly's twin, but her face was narrower, her eyes brown, and her figure slimmer under her shorts and halter top.

She squinted at me. "Do I know you?"

"Name's Percy Carson. I enjoyed talking with Molly, and I'm concerned she hasn't been around."

"I'm Marti, Molly's older sister. She's visiting our sick mother." She looked away, her fingers fidgeting with her shorts. "I'll tell her you asked about her."

"Do you expect her back soon?"

"Why?"

"Ah, no reason."

"Guess it depends on mom. I need to call and check on her."

"Well, better get going. Tell Molly hello."

"Yeah." She turned back to the car.

That night, dressed in jeans and a black sweatshirt, I drove to within a mile of the trailer and parked my SUV behind a hunting camp.

I hiked through the woods, keeping within sight of the road, and using the moonlight to navigate the brush. At the clearing, I stopped. Jake's truck stood in front. No sign of the Pontiac. I knelt and waited, swatting mosquitoes from my face.

About eight-thirty, the lights clicked off. Jake came outside and drove off.

After the truck disappeared, I crossed over his lawn. My boots crunched on the dry grass, my heartbeat increasing with each step. I reached the door and knocked. No answer. I knocked again. Pulled on the handle. Locked.

The sound of a vehicle made me turn. A dark Buick pulled even with the trailer, then swept by me. I pulled out a key and pretended to fumble with the lock.

Wiping sweat from my forehead, I circled to the back. A rusting oil barrel stood about ten feet behind the trailer. Pushing it under the center window, I hiked myself up and grabbed the sill.

The barrel tilted, then toppled. I fell and twisted my ankle. Pain radiated up my leg.

Gritting my teeth, I righted the barrel and climbed back up. I had to get inside that trailer.

I shined my light through the window. A Formica table with three chairs stood in the center of the kitchen, empty beer bottles stacked on the table.

I pulled on the screen. It gave, so I dropped it to the ground. I stuck my head inside and flashed my light around. Plastic microwave containers and dirty pans were stacked in the sink. I smelled burned grease.

A motor sounded from the road. I froze. Lights flashed as a vehicle passed and disappeared down the road.

Leaning in the window, I wiggled my shoulders and pushing with my legs, fell through. The living room had a love seat fronted by a cigarette-scarred coffee table.

I gimped to the back of the trailer. Bed sheets lay on the floor. Opening the accordion doors to the closet, I looked inside. Jeans and men's shirts hung from hooks on the right side, female stuff on the left. On the floor of the closet stood three sets of boots, each one caked with mud.

I went through the pockets of the women's clothes but they were empty. As I pulled open the top dresser drawer, lights flashed across the front window and stopped. Jake's back.

I dashed for the back window, ignoring the protest of my ankle. A door slammed. I propelled myself through the window into the darkness below. My shoulder erupted in pain when I hit a rock.

Forcing myself up, I hobbled toward the woods.

Lights came on in the trailer. A voice yelled, "What the hell?" The beam from his flashlight bounced around the corner of the trailer.

"Hold it, bastard." A round of buckshot tore through the brush, missing me by inches.

I tore through a tangle of vines and brush, thorns ripping at my skin. My leg throbbed with pain.

Another round of buckshot.

I blindly pushed branches from my face, trying to run for the road. The bobbing light gained on me.

Headlights pierced the darkness.

I yelled, "Help."

The vehicle rolled past.

Another round of buckshot rattled the leaves next to me. I pulled up short. Forced myself to stand still.

Jake broke through the last of the vines and flashed the light in my face. "It's you. The nosy jogger. Who the hell do you think you are?"

The glare in my eyes made it tough to think. Sweat poured down my back. "Your wife's missing. Anything happens to me, the cops are going to want to see her."

He motioned with the gun toward the trailer. "Git going."

"The police know I'm here."

"Crap. Nobody's gonna care if I put a round of buckshot into you. You broke into my trailer. I got your scrawny ass dead to rights."

"If I refuse?"

"I'll fill you full of shot right here. Now move."

I limped along the edge of the road. Pain burned up my leg.

The twelve-gauge jabbed my back whenever I slowed. We reached the trailer. "Get inside."

I stumbled up the two steps. Opened the door.

"Over there in the corner." He pointed. "Sit your ass down."

I limped to the couch.

A car pulled up in front. A moment later, the door opened. Marti scowled when she saw me. "Him again. What's he doing here?"

"Nosy bastard. Found him going through the trailer."

Forcing a weak smile I said, "Marti, thank heavens you're here. Tell him I mean no trouble." I looked at Jake. "Look, I worried about Molly. I should have minded my own business." Struggling up from the couch, I stammered, "I'll take off now and won't bother you again."

Jake kept the shotgun pointed at me. "Nice try. You wanted involved. Now you are." He looked at Marti. "What are you going to do with him?"

"What do you think? He threatens me. Fortunately my gun's nearby. Didn't mean to kill him, but it's dark."

I jerked back. "No, please."

Jake glanced at me, then nervously shuffled his feet. "We don't have to kill him, do we?"

Marti pulled a .38 from behind her back and shot Jake twice through the forehead, throwing him against the wall. Noise exploded in my ears, blood splattered the walls.

She turned the gun toward me. "All you men are the same. Weak."

My ears rang. "Why are you doing this?"

"None of your business." She waved the pistol. "All right, outside."

When I pulled open the door, she lifted the gun for a second to grab for the door. I raised my fist and knocked her arm, then tumbled into the darkness.

She was on me like a fly on manure. "That's it, go ahead and run. It'll make my job easier."

"This is murder."

"Wrong. I'm just defending myself."

My leg was on fire.

"Now, you gonna grab that sporting chance and run, or am I gonna shoot you right here? Don't make no difference to me." She grinned. "I'll tell them you shot Jake, then tried to rape me. Pot of stew spilled on the stove, caught fire, and the whole trailer went up in flames."

Maybe she'd miss if I ran. For sure, she'd finish the job here.

Lights moved up the road toward us.

"Stand still," she snarled. "Make a noise. I'll kill you."

The headlights angled in toward the trailer. A red light flashed on top of the car and a search light blinded us. John Williamson's voice boomed over a speaker. "Drop the gun."

Another car pulled in from the opposite direction, another flashing red light.

"Okay, okay," she shouted. "Don't shoot. I'm only defending myself." She dropped the gun. "He shot my brother-in-law and tried to assault me. I think he did something to my sister. She's missing."

Williamson stood behind his car door. "Turn around and face the trailer."

A trooper stepped out of the second car. He picked up the gun and patted down Marti.

"Get your goddamn hands off me. He tried to make time with my sister, rape me."

Williamson called, "Stand still."

The trembling started in my gut. It spread like an ocean wave through my body. I sank to the ground and threw up. Noises exploded through my brain. Everything went fuzzy. Light flickered in and out, then nothing.

I floated to the surface, opened my eyes. An IV pumped fluids into my left arm, my right leg hung suspended from a pole at the end of the bed.

The door opened. John Williamson peeked in. "How ya feeling?"

"Like crap. Have I been out long?"

"Since last night." He sipped from a cup in his right hand, while handing me one with his left. "From the gang at the coffee shop. Last night the EMTs had to wrap your leg and shoulder. Your body looked like a road map from the scratches. I told them to take this dummy to the hospital. He'd never be smart enough to do it himself."

I took a swallow. "Thanks."

"We found the wife, Molly, buried in that patch of earth like you thought. Good thing because Marti swore you killed her sister, then attacked her."

I winced. My stomach did a flip-flop and my tongue felt thick. "Why did they kill her?"

"The two were having an affair. Must have been for insurance money. Marti was a beneficiary on the insurance if anything happened to Jake and Molly. Jake told her about you hanging around. Guess they figured they could blame you."

"I owe you, buddy."

"Looks like they planned to dig Molly up and place her body in the trailer, then set it on fire. Another day and all the evidence would have gone up in smoke."

I shuddered. "How did you know?"

Williamson took another sip of coffee. "A neighbor called dispatch about 9:30 last night and reported hearing shots up on Smith Road. I remembered your creature of habit story and thought I'd better check."

"Next time I'm gonna keep on jogging."

Williamson looked at me from under those bushy eyebrows. "There's still one thing I don't understand."

I started to relax. "What's that?"

"We called and checked on Molly. She left her mother's house after two days. That's over a week ago. Then you know what? I found this letter hidden under some papers in one of the desk drawers."

My gut tightened.

"It's addressed to you. Apparently you knew this Molly pretty well—"

During Don Helin's time in the military, he spent seven years in the Pentagon. Those assignments provide the background for his thrillers. Don's novel, Thy Kingdom Come, *was published in March 2009. His latest thriller,* Devil's Den *is due out this fall.*

For more information go to his website donhelin.com.

12389780R00104

Made in the USA
Charleston, SC
01 May 2012